In the Waiting

One Revolutionary War woman's search for purpose in the midst of her waiting

Molly Kay

Dove Christian
Publishers

A Division of Kingdom Christian Enterprises
PO Box 611
Bladensburg, MD 20710-0611

Copyright 2024 by Molly Hake

All rights reserved.

This novel is a work of fiction. Names, characters, places, and incidents either are products of the author's imagination or are used fictitiously. Any resemblance to actual events or locales or persons, living or dead, is entirely coincidental.

The views, opinions, and actions expressed in this novel are those of the characters and do not necessarily reflect the official policy or position of any person or entity mentioned within. Any resemblance to real persons, living or dead, or actual events is purely coincidental.

No part of this work may be reproduced or transmitted in any form or by any means, electronic or mechanical, including photocopying and recording, or by any information storage or retrieval system, except as may be expressly permitted by the 1976 Copyright Act or in writing from the publisher. Requests for permission can be addressed to Dove Christian Publishers, P.O. Box 611, Bladensburg, MD 20710-0611, www.dovechristianpublishers.com.

Paperback ISBN 978-1-957497-36-5

Inscript and the portrayal of a pen with script are trademarks of Dove Christian Publishers.

Printed in the United States of America

To Nicholas Porges
The one for whom I waited

Special thanks to
Kurt Hake
Who helped me edit and polish this book
to what it is now

Autumn, 1778

Setauket, Long Island

Chapter 1

"Charlotte! Charlotte!"

I restrained myself from responding to my young sister's call in more haste than would befit a lady, but it is hard to contain one's enthusiasm when a long-expected letter arrives.

"Yes, Mary Ann?" I answered with more composure than I felt as I laid aside the book on treating stomach illnesses that I had borrowed from my father's library. I looked towards the doorway of the front parlor where my sister paused just long enough to grab a letter opener from the writing desk before rushing to the settee where I waited.

"This letter came for you just now." She shoved it into my hand along with the opener, which caught on my skirt and tore a hole in it.

"Now look what you've done," I scolded. But I wanted to open the letter just as much as Mary Ann wanted to watch me do so, so I moved on quickly without paying much heed to the gash.

"Thomas said it was sent some time ago, but the mail was delayed because the British army stopped the boat crossing from New York to search for spies carrying messages. I certainly hope they caught any aboard to make it worth the delay." Mary Ann returned her focus to the letter. "I wouldn't have seen it before you," she continued, "but I was waiting by the door for Thomas to return with the mail since I am expecting a letter from Ellen Barlow.

You know she, my best friend, has left me alone here for nearly a month now? I still can't forgive Father for keeping me home while her father is letting her have all the fun in New York. It simply isn't fair. Well?"

I didn't pay much attention to my sister's prattling since I had heard this complaint many times in the previous weeks. I was tired of reminding her that Ellen was two years older than she, that Mary Ann would have her turn in society when Father felt she was ready, and that there was no use complaining since he wasn't likely to change his mind, though Mother was no doubt doing her best to fight for every opportunity that might give her two daughters a chance to make good matches. Certainly, that was why Mother had taken such an interest in Lieutenant Lawerance Taylor. She seemed more excited at the prospect of him and me forming an attachment than even I. Only at Mary Ann's inquiry did I remember that I still had not read the letter, so distracted was I with hoping and guessing its contents.

"It is from Lieutenant Taylor, is it not?" It felt as if she was shouting as she leaned into my ear.

"Shhh, keep your voice down!" I whispered through my teeth, "I don't need the whole house imagining whatever you are. Remember what happened when Mr. Lark stopped calling on me the Christmas before last, despite you having convinced everyone he would propose within days? Or what happened with Mr. Smith? I never saw him again after you and mother scared him off by asking how many children he wanted." Mary Ann apologized, but rolled her eyes, showing me that she was sure this time would be different.

"Yes, it is from Lieutenant Taylor," I replied after giving the letter a quick scan, "and there is nothing of significance to report, so you may be on your way." I

IN THE WAITING

started to fold the letter. I had no desire to read it more intently in the presence of such a nosy sister. I had read enough to know there would be little in it to bring me joy or excitement.

"Oh please, Charlotte, please tell me what he says. Perhaps it will help cure the boredom I have from being left here in sleepy Setauket, too young to enter society while all the other girls my age are either in New York or preparing for the Barlow's autumn ball."

"I am afraid all I can say is that Lieutenant Taylor has been further delayed in his work with the British army in New York and will not return before the ball as he had hoped." I was more disappointed than I was willing to show. I knew Mary Ann would exaggerate whatever she imagined I felt. She did not need to know that I really did have hopes for a future with Lawrence and that I feared this was just a step towards his ending our relationship. He must have heard about my family's precarious financial situation and thought better of his advances.

"He waited nearly three weeks to send you a letter and that is all he says? Whatever are you going to do?" Mary Ann was clearly dejected by the idea that the situation seemed to be the same as what happened with Mr. Lark.

"There is nothing to do," I replied. "He is there, and I am here, and that is that. Now go wash for dinner. Mrs. Phillips will be announcing supper any minute, and Mother and Father will be waiting for us in the drawing room." When my sister had left, I took a moment to consider what the letter meant in the immediate. It meant I would be unable to attend the ball without looking like a desperate old maid, for that would be the general consensus among the gossips if I arrived with only my father to escort me. It also meant I would once again be made to wait.

Waiting seemed to be my lot in life. I had waited a

full seven years for a sister. I had waited to enter society until I was almost seventeen because my family was busy preparing for and making the move from England to the colonies the two years prior. And now I was still waiting for an offer of marriage at age twenty-two, well past the age of many brides. It was not that I was disliked or undesirable. In fact, I was told that my gold hair, fair skin, green eyes, and graceful air were considered by most to make me at least pretty, yet I did not seem to hold the interest of anyone for any length of time. Just as I would begin to feel close to someone, I would discover I did not have as high a place in his heart and mind as he had in mine. Mary Ann would be presented next season, if she could behave herself long enough for Father to consider her ready for such a step, and here I was, a young woman whom everyone seemed to think well of, but whom no one cared to truly befriend.

The chime of the clock brought me back to reality from my bout of self-pity, and I sighed to myself thinking how perfectly selfish I was to be thinking such things when clearly Lawrence was doing his best to finish his business in New York. After all, he did say in his letter that he missed me and was sorry. As much as I wished to escape to my room to sort out my feelings and disappointment instead of attending the evening meal, I knew that would be impossible, as my father had a guest who would be joining the family table. I stood up and smoothed my skirts.

When I found the newly made hole in the fabric, I regretted not taking the advice I gave Mary Ann to clean up a bit before supper, as a guest I had never met would be there. I would have to hope the folds hid the tear, for a late arrival to a meal would cause my mother even greater frustration than an imperfect appearance, and my

IN THE WAITING

mother's frustration was not something I desired to have directed towards me.

I walked into the drawing room only a minute before our housekeeper, Mrs. Phillips, did, so the introductions were brief.

"Charlotte," my father said as the gentlemen rose and the gaze of the room fell on me, "I would like you to meet Mr. Eric Kingsley. Mr. Kingsley, may I present my eldest daughter, Miss Charlotte Devonshire." I was surprised to learn he was our guest, as I recognized the name. He was the son of an old friend of my father. The Kingsleys had moved to Boston from England back before my father had married, so I had never met Eric Kingsley or his parents. Political unrest, and then the war, had kept my family, except Father, on Long Island or in New York City since we moved.

"I am glad to meet you, Miss Devonshire." He took a step towards me and bowed low. He paused there and tilted his head up, revealing a sly grin and a twinkle in his gray eyes before straightening. I hastened to adjust my skirt. He must have seen the hole! How rude of him to acknowledge it like that! Did he have no sense of civility? I fidgeted uncomfortably, but he was awaiting my response.

"A pleasure to make your acquaintance," I replied quickly and took the opportunity to check my dress once more as I curtsied, "We have waited to meet you for so long. Any friend of my father is someone I am happy to know." I don't know why I said the last bit, for it most certainly wasn't true. Father had many young men work with him who seemed rather roguish for being welcomed into a proper English home. But I always seemed to talk more when I was embarrassed or uncomfortable. Mr. Kingsley's solid jaw and wavy brown hair did not help my situation as I was typically most uneasy around handsome men. "I am sorry I am late," I apologized as I turned to my father.

"She has received a letter from Lieutenant Taylor!" Mary Ann blurted quickly.

Apparently she thought an explanation for my delay was necessary.

Thankfully, at that moment Mrs. Phillips entered, and Mother quickly took Father's arm and followed him into the dining room to distract from the outburst. Mr. Kingsley followed suit by taking my arm. He leaned close to my ear, "It must have been some letter to excite you enough to cause a tear in your skirt." I gasped wide eyed but had no chance to reply as we were already taking our places at the table.

Father sat at the head with Mother at his right. Mr. Kingsley was seated at his left with myself beside him and Mary Ann across from me. The meal would have passed quite pleasantly if the gentlemen had talked while the ladies sat silently, as was our normal practice, but Mr.

Kingsley seemed determined to cause me discomfort by harassing me with questions.

"Miss Devonshire, have you learned to like America since your arrival? Though I know that was some time ago now. How do the men of the colonies compare to your suitors in England, for no doubt you had many?" He bowed his head to take a bite of food and looked sideways at me so only I could see the mischievous twinkle his eyes held.

I sat stunned, but Father laughed good naturedly.

"I'm sorry, sir," Mother interjected, "why do you ask such a question?" She seemed as vexed as she was stunned.

Father tried to explain. "Oh, darling, Mr. Kingsley is simply being friendly. He is no stranger here and should

IN THE WAITING

not feel as though he must behave as such."

Father may have felt this way because he had spent a brief time with the Kingsley family in Massachusetts shortly after our move, but to the rest of us, who had only met the young Mr. Kingsley that day, he *was* a stranger.

"Oh, I am sorry if I have overstepped, ma'am. I meant no offense. Mr. Devonshire is right. I am afraid I have not spent very much time in high society recently. I meant only that your daughter has reason to have had many admirers. But again, I apologize, Mrs. Devonshire, Miss Devonshire."

"I understand, and apologize for misreading what you meant by it," conceded Mother, but she did not seem to understand and was certainly no more comfortable with Mr. Kingsley's style of conversation now than she had been before.

"There is nothing to apologize for," I replied, "I have heard the colonists are rather… apathetic to things like reputation and respectability, so it is not your fault if they have influenced you in that way."

No one said a word for some time, and as I realized how harsh my comment was, the sting of it likely hurt me more than it had Mr. Kingsley. I had only meant to repay a bit of the teasing he had given me. I didn't mean to insult his character. No wonder no man had ever remained in my life long enough to marry me. I was an expert at saying the wrong thing at the wrong time. Yet to apologize now would be impossible. I just smiled as sweetly as I could, hoping he would take it as a joke, and turned my attention to the food in front of me.

He returned my smile with another question. "And Miss Devonshire," he began just as I took a bite of a much too hot potato to distract from the inner guilt of what I had said. I struggled to keep it in my mouth.

"Do you enjoy dancing?" He did not sound as lighthearted as before. He almost sounded cold, like he was speaking only out of the necessity to move on from what had just transpired between us. Then he added under his breath, "Perhaps that is what has caused the tear in your dress." I nearly choked. I glanced at my mother and saw that she still did not appreciate such questions being asked of her daughter by a man I had just met, but also that she had thankfully not heard his second comment.

"Well," I began hesitantly but defiantly after I had swallowed, forgetting all regret I had for my previous statement, "I find dancing an enjoyable diversion on such occasions that call for it and when there are *gentlemen* with whom to share it." Eric's eyes narrowed at the insinuation of my remark, but my mother's face relaxed. I could tell she was satisfied that I gave an answer that did not invite further discussion and discouraged any other seemingly advancive comments Mr. Kingsley may have considered directing towards me. My mother need not have worried. I had no interest in this long-lost family friend who was too forward and crass to be considered a true gentleman. I would hope I could set my sights higher than that. I was sure Mr. Kingsley had no real interest in me as anything more than the object of a good tease anyway, especially after what I had said.

I was unaware of the awkwardness of the silence that followed my second, admittedly rude, comment until it was made worse by Mary Ann. "How sad you must be that you don't have anyone to take you to the autumn ball now that Lieutenant Taylor will not be here!"

"Mary Ann!" My mother gave her a sharp look of reproof for speaking out of turn with such personal information, then turned to me with questions in her eyes.

"Oh?" my father exclaimed, "Well, I am sorry to hear

IN THE WAITING

the Lieutenant will not be joining us at Fencomb, but I am sure Charlotte will not be required to stay behind. Someone will surely be willing to escort her, especially if I ask." My cheeks flushed red with embarrassment. I may be behind when it came to securing a man and a stable future, but I did not need my father to find someone to take me to a ball. "Why, young Kingsley, you must come to the ball. I am sure our invitation from the Barlows may be extended to you. And as I have just invited you, you cannot already have asked someone to the ball. Would you be so kind as to escort Charlotte to the dance?"

I wished I could have run out of the room and never seen Eric Kingsley again. The whole group held its breath for Mr. Kingsley's response, even Mr. Kingsley.

"I suppose as a *gentleman* I must oblige." His emphasis on the word did not go unnoticed, certainly not by the one who had more than implied his being unworthy of such a title. "Miss Devonshire, would you do me the honor of allowing me to escort you to the autumn dance this Friday?"

I knew I was right in my previous judgment of this insufferable man. My first instinct was to refuse with a stinging remark, but then I remembered that Mary Ann did have a point. This was the only way I could go to the dance that I had looked forward to for weeks. Despite my tendency for embarrassment in society, I did still enjoy social functions, especially those with dancing, which, along with reading medical journals, was a favorite pastime of mine, though I would never tell Mr. Kingsley so. I made a decision then that though I would have to accept, I would make Mr. Kingsley regret his insulting behavior. It was either that or I would have to tag along with my parents.

"Why yes, I would be flattered to be escorted by a

gentleman such as you, sir." I managed to give my answer with enough spite to satisfy my malicious desires for the moment. My reply seemed to frustrate him as if he had intentionally asked me in the least inviting way possible.

Though that idea angered me, it made me glad to see I had succeeded even so slightly in making him wish he had not provoked me.

"It's settled then!" Father concluded, rising from the table and not seeming to notice the obvious reluctance with which both parties had agreed to his solution. "And the two of you will have plenty of time to become acquainted with one another as I have invited Mr. Kingsley to stay with us here at Longford until his family returns from their trip to England, which with the war will most likely be some time. He has had to stay behind for business reasons, you see, as I have asked him to assist me in some matters."

It was not uncommon for my father to have men stay for a few days while working with him, but I somehow knew this would be different. My father was all too eager to pair me with him for the dance. It seemed Mr. Kingsley would not be leaving anytime soon.

When we had finished eating, we adjourned to the drawing room. The two men stood by the fire, and we ladies sat on the sofas as we conversed.

"So, Mr. Kingsley, have you heard any recent news of the war?" Mother must have been desperate to turn his attention away from me if she was willing to bring up the war.

"Well, Mrs. Devonshire, since gaining such support from the French, the colonists are putting up a formidable fight."

"It's meddling, if you ask me," chimed Mother, "The French just want an excuse to stab us in the back."

"Miss Devonshire, what do *you* think about the

IN THE WAITING

colonists' use of the French?" He looked at me expectantly, as if he was trying to uncover something.

"Lieutenant Taylor thinks that it reveals a lack of confidence and backbone to be relying on France."

"With all due respect, Miss Devonshire, I asked what you think, not what your Lieutenant thinks."

My mother's attempt had failed in sparing me from his harassment. My cheeks flushed hot and I scrambled for something smart to say. '*My* Lieutenant'... The audacity of this man!

"Well, personally, I do not think the French would support a group that is weak enough to doom them to failure. They are too smart for that… At least that is what I heard Andrew Barlow say last we visited Fencomb," I hastened to say for fear my mother would think me insolent.

Eric didn't reply but only shook his head. No one knew what to say next, so we sat in the quiet, listening to the crackling of the fire and the wind outside for a moment.

I couldn't pretend I was enjoying our guest any longer. I excused myself from the room but did not escape his presence, as he also decided to retire and followed me out.

When we were safely in the hall, I heard from behind, "Miss Devonshire, may I speak to you for a moment?"

I turned to face him and nodded though I had no desire to hear what he had to say.

"You don't like me, and, quite frankly, I'm beginning to reciprocate the feeling," he said matter of factly. "So if you would rather not go to the dance with me, I am sure I could take the disappointment." I couldn't believe what I was hearing. Not that I doubted the truth of his words, but I couldn't believe he was actually saying them to me, and with such sarcasm!

"No doubt there are still one or two men out there who

would be desperate enough to take you. You certainly strike me as the kind of woman who wouldn't mind the whole town knowing that the last pick of the crop was the best escort she could get for a high class ball."

I could hold my tongue no longer. "Oh! And you don't care one lick what people think of you? Is that it? We'll see about that. Mr. Kingsley," I held my nose high, my cheeks hot as fire, "I said I would go with you and I will, but I promise you; you will regret how you have treated me. You, sir, are no gentleman, so do not be surprised if I refuse to treat you as such!" I appreciated the look of frustration on his face before I spun on my heel and rushed up the stairs, at the top of which I saw Mary Ann had been waiting, thankfully out of earshot.

"I suppose you won't be as lonely without Lawrence now that another young man is here," she whispered mischievously. I could have smacked her had I not been so shocked by the remark that she had time to escape my reach.

Did everyone see me as being so desperate as to need a man so beneath me to be begged to take me to the dance and live in my family's house?

Chapter 2

The two days leading to the ball thankfully passed rather uneventfully. Mr. Kingsley evidently had business of my father to attend to that kept him busy much of the time, so we only saw each other at meals. He had stopped asking such personal questions, and it seemed he considered our conversation an agreement of a truce of some kind because he only spoke to me when absolutely necessary.

When the night of the autumn ball came, though I had wished with all my heart something like a dreadful illness would prevent me from arriving on the arm of a man I despised so much, I had the misfortune of being in perfect health. Mary Ann would take my place in a heartbeat, I was sure, but alas, she wished to go but had to stay, and I wished to stay but had to go. As my mother reminded me whenever she had the chance, since I had no brothers, it was my duty to marry well so that she, Mary Ann, and myself would be provided for. I did not have the luxury of turning down the opportunity to be in society. Normally I would have no desire to miss such a grand event, but attending a dance with a high-class gentleman like Lieutenant Taylor was very different from being escorted by Mr. Eric Kingsley.

I looked in the mirror one more time. Maggie, who had been Mary Ann's and my maid since we first came to the colonies, was helping me get ready. "Oh, this won't do," I told her, as she tried to put a string of pearls around my neck. "Use these." I lifted my best green jewels from the armoire. "They match my dress and bring out my eyes. I need to look my absolute best, and arriving with Mr. Kingsley won't do me any favors. You know what my mother always says, 'Always present your best when there are men to impress.' Though normally that irritates me, I'm inclined to agree tonight."

"Yes, miss, I'll do my best, miss. Your father told me to help you look particularly beautiful tonight."

"He did? Why, whatever for? He has never seemed to like mother's encouraging me to 'catch men.'" I adjusted the ruffles on the skirt of my gown as I thought. "He can't possibly... no, he can't *still* be hoping Mr. Kingsley and I..." I didn't finish the thought. It was simply too ridiculous.

"I don't know, miss, but you did say he seemed awful quick in suggesting Mr. Kingsley take ya tonight."

"Yes. He did."

"Well, that Mr. Kingsley isn't *too* bad to look at, if you don't mind me sayin'."

"Of course, he isn't bad-looking! He's one of the best-looking men I've ever seen! That's what makes it so terrible! He hates me so it is all for nothing. Besides, I don't care for him either. He is rude and forward and a tease. He deserves no more respect from me than what he has given to me." I spun around, grabbed my fur coat and gloves from Maggie's hands, and left the room. I made my way down the steps, trying to cool my temper on the way to where the rest of the party was waiting for the carriage to be brought around.

"Why, you look lovely, my dear! Doesn't she look lovely?" Father exclaimed and turned to Mr. Eric Kingsley, who politely agreed with a simple nod and smile. Though this question gave credit to the idea that Father was

IN THE WAITING

attempting to kindle a relationship between Mr. Kingsley and me, I could not help but beam at my father's praise. I knew my purpose was to secure an advantageous marriage, and since I had so far been unsuccessful in this pursuit, I greatly appreciated praise. Each bit that I was given gave me the confidence I needed to carry myself with patience for a little while longer. Perhaps I did rely too much on praise as Mr. Kingsley had implied. But it was praise that gave me hope for any sort of success in my life, so what was there to be ashamed of in seeking it out? After all, there would be no way I could marry well if I did not pay attention to what people thought of me.

Mr. Kingsley helped me with my coat, and we all stepped outside. I was glad Maggie had insisted I wear my fur coat instead of the light one I had first chosen. The weather was quite frigid this late in November. Eric helped me into the carriage and sat beside me. I did not need to worry about conversing with the man next to me as my parents, who sat across from us, kept the chatter going as they discussed the people Eric would meet at the dance. I did, however, worry about what to say to him for the rest of the evening when there would be no escaping the need to talk to him. I had the skills a lady needed to politely converse with gentlemen, but Eric did not follow the usual rules of etiquette and decorum when it came to conversation, as he had shown at our family dinner. I chastised myself for not having prepared a list of things to talk about or ways to respond if ever he asked me something I felt I could not answer.

"Charlotte?"

I had not noticed that my mother was asking me a question. "Yes? Forgive me, Mother, I was lost in thought."

My father studied me with concern, but Eric's gaze was one of amusement. It was the same look he had given me when he noticed my torn dress. Oh, I hated how much enjoyment he seemed to get from my embarrassment.

"I was just telling Mr. Kingsley about Andrew and Edward Barlow. Of course, Edward is the younger and is married to Sarah, but it is rumored that Andrew has intention for the Church, is it not so? Which, of course, will leave the estate to Edward since their father has passed."

"I believe that is what their sister Ellen told Mary Ann last we discussed it." "Excellent!" Mr. Kingsley replied, "Then everyone must be on their best behavior, since they will be in front of a soon-to-be minister." He looked at me in such a way as if to dare me to try anything.

Did he have no sense? It was then that I had my idea of how to both rid myself of this man's presence for the evening as well as pay him back for his continued lack of decorum and civility. The first chance I got, I would introduce him to Ada Winters. If he didn't think he cared about what other people thought of him, and that everyone would be on their best behavior tonight, he was sorely mistaken, for Ada was the most obnoxious flirt on the island and would certainly test both of Mr. Kingsley's claims.

When our carriage arrived at the front steps of Fencomb, Eric helped me down and took my arm as we followed my parents to the ballroom of the manor. It was just as beautiful as I had hoped. Since the French joined the war on the side of the rebels, parties such as these were becoming less and less common, so each one was an event to be treasured. The ceilings were higher than I remembered from last year, and the room much larger. It stretched from the front of the house to the back and so had two walls of windows on opposite sides through which the moonlight shone. There were elaborate settees and chairs around the room and a large space cleared for dancing in the middle. The band was situated under the farther wall of windows.

Mrs. Barlow and her two sons greeted us at the double door entrance. "Thank you for having us tonight," my mother said.

"It is always a pleasure to host fellow neighbors still loyal to the crown," added Edward Barlow. My father smiled and shook his hand, but I thought I felt Eric's arm in mine get tense.

"Now brother, we know you have been proud of the king's victories and frustrated with his opponents of late, but we have promised Mother there would be no talk of the war tonight. It's wonderful to see you again, Sir." Andrew shook my father's hand then turned to Mr.

Kingsley. "And I am so glad to have you join our party this evening, as well."

"Thank you, Sir, I am grateful for your hospitality," Eric answered and shook Andrew's hand as we removed our coats.

Mrs. Barlow gave me a warm smile. "Welcome, dear. I believe Sarah is sitting across the room somewhere. She has been eager to see you. Have a wonderful evening," she said. Eric began leading me in the direction Mrs. Barlow had gestured.

I spotted Sarah conversing with a few ladies I did not recognize, but when she saw me approach, she excused herself from their company and hurried to welcome us.

"Charlotte! Oh, I am so happy you have come!" Lady Barlow was two years younger than I, but she had at one time been a friend to me like Ellen was to Mary Ann. She had done so much to help me fit into society when we first arrived on Long Island. Though, naturally, our different positions in life, her being married and I not, had put an unintentional distance in our friendship over the past couple of years, I still very much enjoyed her company.

"I am happy to be here and happy to see you," I answered with genuine pleasure. "May I introduce Mr. Kingsley, a guest of my family. And, Mr. Kingsley, this is Lady Sarah Barlow, Sir Edward's wife."

"A pleasure to meet you, ma'am," said Eric.

"Likewise, sir." Sarah curtsied. "What brings you to Setauket?"

"My family lives in Boston, but when my parents decided to wait out the rest of the war in England, it was decided I should stay with our friends, the Devonshires, instead of going with them. I am in business with Mr. Devonshire."

"Oh! Well, your family's loss is our gain," she responded with a coy smile, "And what kind of business would that be?" She tried to act natural, but it appeared she was going beyond the usual pleasantries and toward intense interest.

"Just business," Eric smiled back, then rose. "May I have this dance?" he inquired, offering his hand to me.

"Yes, thank you," I replied, standing clumsily. I had not expected the conversation to end so abruptly.

"It has been an honor making your acquaintance, Lady Barlow," Eric said to Sarah as he bowed. She nodded, but Sarah's curiosity seemed to have been piqued. I admit even I was a little intrigued. My father had never shared much about his business dealings. I had always assumed he was just dealing with our farmland and investments and such. I could not think of why Eric wouldn't be able to explain as much to Sarah. Perhaps he simply didn't want to take the time or effort. I did not have time to ponder long, as we were lining up with the other couples, the music was

IN THE WAITING

starting, and we were beginning the dance.

"Is your father interested in medicine?" Eric evidently, and unfortunately, *was* going to follow the rules of polite conversation tonight and insist on talking while we danced.

"Not particularly so. Why?"

"I saw a book on broken bones in the parlor yesterday."

"He collects books of all kinds." I did not give a further explanation though I knew he was waiting for it.

"*You* are the one reading it," he exclaimed with surprise. It seemed he had only needed to look at me to discover this fact.

We had to separate to take our turn weaving around the other couples, but when we came back together, he continued.

"I must say I am surprised. I had you figured as an entitled heiress too stuck up to be anything of substance. But this does explain things."

"How so?" I asked with genuine curiosity as I stepped around him.

"It explains why you aren't married yet, despite your obvious obsession with becoming so."

My face flamed hot. How dare he. I stiffened my jaw and squared my shoulders. "And what do you mean by that, *sir*," I spat the title with as much sarcasm as I dared, but under my breath. The last thing I needed was for the people who surrounded us to hear what he had to say.

He appeared to be unperturbed by my obvious discomfort and frustration. "Well, none of these men would want a wife with such tendencies towards intelligent reading and conversation." He gestured to the room, and in my mind, I conceded that he was right. "They must be intimidated by you," he continued, so matter-of-factly that I almost believed he was serious. But I knew such an absurd notion could not be thought true. Besides, Mr. Kingsley had made his negative opinion of me clear enough that I could never trust an evaluation he gave of me or of what people thought of me.

I didn't know how to respond, so we finished the dance in silence. When we had applauded the band, Eric led me to where my mother and Mrs. Barlow were sitting together against the wall near the front windows.

"Now if you will excuse me, I have someone with whom I must speak," and Eric bowed slightly, spun on his heel, and crossed to the opposite end of the wall of glass.

Chapter 3

"You dance as wonderfully as ever, my dear," Mrs. Barlow complimented me, as I took a seat beside her.

"Thank you, Mrs. Barlow." I spied through the crowd and saw Eric had found Father and Andrew Barlow.

"Yes, though I am afraid you are stumbling more than usual with this new partner of yours," added my mother.

"Tell me, Mrs. Barlow," I continued, ignoring my mother's remark, "Will Mr. Barlow be joining the Church soon?"

"Why yes, as a matter of fact, he has begun studying via correspondence with a seminary professor and shall be shadowing a minister at a small church in town. Of course, I shall still be seeing you in our church. As a societal leader I cannot leave the congregation, but I think this church will suit his needs for now, especially as Edward has agreed to support him financially for as long as he needs."

"How nice! You must be very proud of your son." I looked back towards the gentleman and had to adjust my position to see that they were looking out the windows across the bay, discussing something.

"And of your son Sir Edward, too," Mother added. "I hear he has been instrumental in the British cause of late."

"I am proud of both my sons, and yes." She beckoned us to lean towards her. "Edward has just been appointed as the civilian in the area responsible for keeping an eye out for any suspicious activity." She put her finger over her mouth to show us that she was not supposed to give that information away, but that she was not at all sorry she did once she saw the result she desired on my mother's astonished face.

"How exciting!" Mother replied. You would have thought Edward was defeating whole armies single-handedly the way she went on. I turned my attention, however, to Mr. Kingsley, Mr. Barlow, and my father, who were now standing very near one another, speaking softly with looks of consternation as if they were solving some great puzzle. But I could not hear them above the clammer of the crowd.

"And I certainly hope this helps end the war soon," Mrs. Barlow was saying, "You would not believe how difficult it was to acquire what we needed for this party… and how expensive!"

"Oh, I am sure, why just the other day in town…"

I did not need to listen to Mother's tale of overpriced ribbon again. I returned to studying Mr. Kingsley. I could not understand him. My father seemed to like him so well, but he did not, in my view, earn this good opinion. Just then he turned and looked at me. I hastened to divert my gaze.

"Are you alright?" my mother asked. "You seem rather preoccupied." "I'm fine," I answered cheerfully. "This is a lovely ball, Mrs. Barlow." "Thank you, Charlotte." She smiled back.

The men had stopped talking, and my father was coming towards us, followed closely by Mr. Kingsley.

"And now, my love," Father said as he offered his hand to his wife when they had reached us, "May I have this dance?"

"Yes, darling, thank you."

IN THE WAITING

"And Mr. Kingsley," he paused before taking the dance floor, "it would make me so happy if you would dance this waltz with Charlotte. I love to see her enjoying herself."

I don't know why Father would think I would enjoy myself when it was Mr. Kingsley I would be dancing with, but once again, my father suggested something, and we had no choice but to oblige. Eric took my hand, led me out, and pulled me to him. He was doing everything in the way he ought, but was rather stiff about it, at least for a moment.

"What were you discussing with my father and Mr. Barlow?" I kept my eyes focused on his crisp, white cravat to avoid his face. I had made up my mind I was more likely to get an answer out of him if he did not know how curious I was. "You seemed quite enamored by the view."

"You are quite right, Miss Devonshire. We were enjoying the view of the bay and of the ships heading to Connecticut."

"It is such a shame it is controlled by the Patriots. I would love to visit Connecticut.

Because of the war, I have barely left the island since our arrival in the colonies."

He spun me around, and we glided across the floor side by side with his arm across my shoulders. He twirled me back to face him with our hands meeting above our heads, then slid his hand down my back to its place on my waist. It sent shivers through me, and I had to catch my breath before I continued my pursuit of information.

"Was there something in your view that concerned you? I hope there was no sign of trouble on the water."

"Yes, as a matter of fact, while I was having my private conversation with Andrew Barlow and your father, I did see something that concerned me." I finally looked up into his eyes to hear his explanation. His face showed worry. "I saw a woman staring at me... as if she was trying to see right through me to discover a dark secret. It was very much like the way you've been trying to see through my coat and shirt these last several minutes." He grinned wickedly, and I quickly looked away, my cheeks flaring.

Thankfully the dance was ending. I could not spend any more time in the arms of this man after that remark. I was more resolved than ever to teach him a lesson. If he did not want to be a gentleman, I would give him what he wanted and prove him wrong on many accounts while I was at it. "Please," I said, gesturing for us to leave the dance floor as the crowd began to applaud the orchestra. "I have someone I would like you to meet."

I scanned the room and found Ada holding a glass of champagne and flirting busily with three or four men. She turned from them when she saw us approach. She had no doubt noticed right away that I had with me a handsome man whom she had not yet had the chance to wrap around her finger.

"Why Charlotte Devonshire! Who *do* you have here? Sir, I simply must know your name." She gave a sample of her irritating cackle. She sounded like a choking chipmunk. I felt I could be sick. I swallowed hard.

"Ada, may I present Mr. Eric Kingsley. Mr. Kingsley, Miss Ada Winters."

"A pleasure to make your acquaintance," Ada said as she stepped forward, much closer than necessary, and offered her hand.

"The pleasure is mine," Eric replied, taking her hand, though not kissing it, as Ada had clearly intended.

Now was the time for me to bow out. "Excuse me, but I need a glass of water." Before Eric could stop me, I was on my way to the other side of the room where I

IN THE WAITING

found a spot from which I could watch Ada do what she did best, reveal the weaknesses of men. As soon as the next song began, Ada had Mr. Kingsley on the dance floor. Ada was so obvious in her flirtations that I almost felt bad for subjecting Eric to such embarrassment. She cackled so noisily and so often that almost everyone in the room had noticed the pair.

"Isn't that the boy escorting Miss Devonshire?" I heard one woman say.

"How embarrassing for such a fine lady to have him as an escort," the eager listener replied. "But then we know Miss Devonshire has had trouble holding onto her better men in the past."

I turned away before I could hear any more of their conversation. Eric was not "my man" and it was none of their business whether or not I could "hold onto" him. But the truth in their statements still hurt, as well as the knowledge that in trying to injure Mr. Kingsley's reputation, I had injured mine even more greatly.

When the song came to a close, I got up to go and rescue him from Ada, and myself from further damage. Besides, I was sure she had had sufficient time to make him realize he did in fact value his reputation enough to be made uncomfortable by her flirtatious ways. I made my way across the great hall, but was too late. I saw Ada leading Eric into the next room, which I knew would be empty. My heart started to race, and I hastened to the door, bumping into several guests in my hurry. I was about to go in and act as if I had stumbled upon them accidentally, but I froze once I caught a glimpse through the open crack in the door. There was Eric, with his hands on Ada's waist and Ada with her arms around his neck, her lips just inches from his. I turned quickly away, heat rising to my cheeks.

How dare he accept such inappropriate advances from

another woman when he is my escort! I thought. *Yes, I wanted to embarrass him, but he isn't embarrassed by Ada's ridiculous flirting at all! He seems to enjoy it...and encourage it! And all I've managed to do is hurt my own prospects.* I could not stand one more minute. I made my way to the other side of the ballroom, where my father and mother were discussing the choice of refreshments with Mrs. Barlow.

"Thank you for a wonderful evening, Mrs. Barlow, but I am afraid we must be off," I said. All three looked not a little confused, for it was quite early in the evening, but none objected as they must have seen that I was rattled and flushed.

"Certainly, dear," she answered, "I'll have your carriage called. Beth," she said to a nearby servant, "go and fetch the Devonshires' coats."

I saw out of the corner of my eye that Mr. Kingsley had come back into the ballroom and that Ada was standing there, from whence he came, watching him striding in the midst of dancing couples towards us. He was drawing even more attention to himself. I turned my back to the room, and when he said my name as he approached, I pretended not to hear, instead busying myself with putting on my coat that the maid had brought. He reached out a hand to help me with a look of concern, but I dodged it and made my way through the foyer to the door. He and my parents followed, after they had paid their respects to the Barlows.

The ride home was more than unpleasant. Thankfully my parents knew better than to ask me questions in front of Mr. Kingsley, and after I had coolly answered Eric's questioning with a feeble, and thoroughly unbelievable, excuse about a headache, he managed to hold his tongue as well. I could see, though, that he was both concerned and confused as to why I seemed so angry with him. The

IN THE WAITING

fact that he could not guess the reason only made me think worse of him.

I escaped to my room as soon as we arrived home, only to be faced with Mary Ann's interrogation about all the particulars of the evening and Maggie's fussing over getting my hair undone and untangled. When I was finally alone in the room, I indulged myself in a cry, not for the foul character of our houseguest, as I had already determined it to be less than worthy, but rather because I couldn't stand the thought that a man like that had proved me wrong. He didn't have pride that caused him to obsess over what other people thought, and I did. If I didn't, I wouldn't have put myself in the situation of having an escort leave me for another woman. On the other hand, his apathy didn't work out any better for him. He had lost any sliver of respect I had managed somehow to hold onto until now. I wallowed in my self-pity and contemplated ways to rectify my miserable social existence. I was sure Mr. Kingsley thought me a selfish fool. If only Lawerence would come home. He always knew how to make me feel loved.

Chapter 4

The next morning, at dawn, I went out for my usual walk before breakfast, feeling much less angry with the world and even holding a glimmer of hope for what the coming Christmas season might bring in regard to the securing of my future. I was thankful the snow had not yet come, but I knew I would not have long to enjoy early walks outside. I decided to go up to the widow's walk on the top of the house to take in the view of the sunrise on what appeared to be the beginning of a beautifully clear day.

There would be a few dinner parties and dances planned with Christmas around the corner, though the war would mean each would be a little less grand than perhaps they had been at one time. As I climbed the steps on the outdoor stairway at the back of the house, being careful not to slip on the frosty steps, I contemplated what I might want to find to wear to each event.

I reached the top and took a deep breath of the cool wind coming off Conscience Bay. Our house sat at the top of a rise. From the front of the widow's walk, which faced northwest, I looked out over the trees in the direction of Setauket Harbor and the town at the water's edge. To the northeast side lay Port Jefferson, which I could see well. As soon we came from England, the widow's walk became my favorite place on the property. I loved to watch the whale boats and other ships coming in and going out as

IN THE WAITING

they crossed from Connecticut to the harbors on Long Island.

I turned to the south, where I could overlook our own orchards as well as the farmland of the properties surrounding ours. Beyond the orchards directly behind us was an unkempt field, past which was an empty house. The estate, called Penningcoll, had been vacated by its owner a year before, when the British army had run all the Patriots off the island following the Battle of Setauket in 1777. I had not known the old man who had lived there very well, as he had kept out of society since before our arrival to the colonies in 1773. All I knew was that he was considered mad by the locals and had been almost eager to be out of his house when the British took hold of the area. It seemed a shame that the beautiful old house stood vacant. I had often wondered where the man had ended up and if he was still alive. I knew he was a Patriot and thus the enemy, but for him to lose everything just didn't feel quite right.

The sun was rising and its warmth felt good on my face. As it became light enough to walk the gardens, I made my way back down and toward the half circle of fir trees and benches that surrounded a small fountain my mother had decided to put in when we purchased Longford. It was another favorite spot of mine, especially in winter, for even when the fountain stopped running, the trees stayed full and engulfed the small alcove with their sweet fragrance.

I sat down on a bench and closed my eyes, holding a soft bough to my nose and picturing myself entering a grand Christmas Eve dinner on the arm of a wealthy and respectable gentleman, with everyone turning to look in admiration. I was so entranced in my daydream that I did not hear the approaching footsteps coming up the path behind me.

"It's a beautiful morning, isn't it?" It was Eric.

My eyes flashed open, and I released the branch from my clasp as heat rushed to my cheeks. I must have looked ridiculous sitting there with my face in a tree.

"It is," I replied, looking towards the east with genuine appreciation for the day. Though it was cold, the sunrise was breathtaking through the barren trees on the edge of the estate. I was too encouraged by the image I had created in my mind a moment before to hold any grudge for Eric's actions the previous night, so I decided I might as well be civil.

"How are you feeling this morning?" he asked.

I turned slightly and saw he was searching my face with sincere concern. I almost felt bad for the cold shoulder I had given him on the ride home.

"I am feeling much better. Thank you."

He looked relieved and took a step towards the bench where I was sitting, and I moved to offer him a seat. We sat watching the sunrise and listening to the wind for a moment in silence. I could not have thought of anything to say, even if I had wanted to.

"Miss Devonshire," he began as he turned to face me, "I cannot help but wonder if I was the cause of your distress last night. I would like to apologize for what I said the other night, degrading your character. I was out of turn. I have given you no reason to like me and so should not be surprised that you don't. And it is not as if we are here for each other's sake. We need not be in one another's company if we do not wish. I should not have let your father pressure me into taking you to the ball when I knew it would upset you. Will you forgive me?"

I hesitated, but then remembered how my animosity had backfired and decided it was not worth the risk. "Of course, and I should have been more understanding of the position he put you in as well. I am quite sorry for what I said myself. I had no right to treat my father's guest and employee in such a manner."

He must have noticed there was more bothering me, for he continued, "Was there something else I said or did to offend you?" Though he was pressing, he did not look like a puppy desperate for approval or acceptance. He was still firm-jawed and upright. It seemed to be a concern for me, rather than a concern for what I thought of him, that drove him to inquire further as to the cause of our hasty removal from the Barlows' ball. I felt I owed him some sort of explanation now that we had exchanged apologies. I let out a quick sigh and sat up a little straighter.

"I suppose I was just…disappointed with the evening." I tried to act cheerful. "I had been looking forward to having Lieutenant Taylor as an escort. Well, I… I shouldn't have expected to make any progress without the Lieutenant there… and yes, I do care what everyone must think of me, especially after last night's failure." Then I added under my breath, "Not only am I not married, I can't even entertain an escort for one evening." I said the last part more to myself than to Eric, but he certainly heard it.

"Oh, but you were very entertaining! After all, it was you who introduced me to Miss Winters." His eyes held a tease of knowing that confused and unnerved me. Why would he allude to the "entertainment" he received from Miss Winters to my face?

"You did not mind that she and I danced? To be quite honest, I could hardly have refused her."

I raised my eyebrows and tried to act surprised at the thought I should mind in the least.

"Me? Mind? Why no, it is none of my business if you want to pay her your respects."

After several minutes of silence he continued, "Your family seems very invested in your love life."

I blushed. "Yes, I am afraid so. But it is their prerogative. After all, my mother and sister are relying on me to make an advantageous match, so that their futures will be secured as well as mine." I sighed and smiled at him weakly.

We sat for a moment, listening to the wind and watching the sun as it took over more of the sky.

"I believe I misunderstood you, Miss Devonshire. To be blunt, I thought you were obsessed over what others think of you because you were vain and proud. I see now that you have been burdened with astounding pressure and expectations that you must live up to. I am sorry you have such a responsibility."

I was shocked! Who was this compassionate and understanding man before me? I struggled to fit this new side I was seeing into my picture of his character, and it came out muddled and confused.

"Thank you for understanding," I began cautiously, "but it is not so bad. I have a purpose and I am determined to live up to it." After another minute, I remarked, "I suppose we should walk back to the house. Breakfast will be served shortly."

About a week after the disastrous ball at Fencomb, I arose to find my window lined with frost and the outside world covered in a thin blanket of glistening snow. It was much too cold for a walk just now. Perhaps it would be warmer after breakfast when the sun had had a chance to shine for a while and thaw the frozen ground.

Breakfast was relatively normal. Normal, that is, for the time since Mr. Kingsley had begun his stay at Longford.

IN THE WAITING

I did start to notice, however, that Eric was not as brash as he had first been. He spoke with more tact than he did at our first meeting, at least when my mother was present. Perhaps she scared him. Though he did not seem like he would scare easily, he did seem smart enough not to intentionally upset his hostess. He had likely only grown wiser in knowing that if he did not want to be the cause of a quarrel between my parents, he would have to put up some front of decorum in the presence of my mother. However, no sooner had I noticed the positive change in him than he showed he had not changed at all.

After the meal, as I left the dining room following my parents, Eric came up behind me and whispered in my ear, "Get dressed in your riding habit and meet me out back in half an hour."

I was still astounded at his forwardness. "Will you?" he asked.

I just looked at him with an empty expression. Going for a planned ride with this man was something entirely different than meeting by chance on walks.

"I'll take that as a yes then." When I opened my mouth to protest, he continued. "There is no use arguing. I won't take no for an answer." He grinned devilishly.

"Eric, my boy," my father called from his chair across the drawing room where he sat reading a letter. "I must speak with you on a matter of business."

"I'll see you in half an hour," he said quietly, then turned to attend my father.

I was not sure what had just happened, but I felt as though something had stirred the waters of our barely amiable acquaintanceship. I didn't think I liked it, but I went up and changed anyway. A ride did sound like a nice idea as walking through the snow was out of the question, but I was determined to keep a close eye on Mr. Kingsley.

After seeing him with Ada, I was sure he was not a man who could be trusted.

I came down a short while later to meet him on the back veranda as he requested, but when I opened the door, Mr. Kingsley stood with only Marble, my horse.

"I am terribly sorry, Miss Devonshire, though you no doubt will not mind in the least, but your father has requested that I attend to some urgent business for him that will unfortunately take me out of town immediately. I am afraid you will have to ride on your own this morning. I beg your pardon."

I tried to hide my relief and replied, "Oh, there is nothing to be sorry for. I know these things happen. I hope it is nothing serious." I had suddenly noticed that he seemed sullen and grave, as if he was bearing the weight of the world. His eyes were much duller than they had been earlier that morning. Perhaps it was the strain of the war. I had seen it take its toll on many men my father worked with. "Don't worry. My father and Lieutenant Taylor are sure we will quelch this rebellion in not too much longer," I assured him.

He did not seem at all comforted by this, but before I could further question his downcast expression, he handed me the reins, bowed slightly, and departed.

༄

I thoroughly enjoyed my ride for I no longer had to share it with Mr. Kingsley. As I entered the house through the door on the back veranda, after returning my horse to the stable hand, I was greeted by a rather hysterical Mary Ann, which was not entirely uncommon.

"Oh, sister!" she exclaimed, rushing towards me. "Ellen has brought the most shocking news! It's Lieutenant Taylor!"

IN THE WAITING

I was at a loss as to what Mary Ann could be trying to say. "What? Slow down. What is going on, Mary Ann?"

"Ellen told me in the letter I received from her just now that Lieutenant Taylor... well... that she... that the Lieutenant has made advances towards her and even escorted her to a party the other night." She searched my face, no doubt looking for heartbreak. Instead, I am sure she saw the anger rising in me as I started rushing up the stairs to my room. She followed closely behind.

"So that is why he couldn't come home to take me to the ball! He just didn't want to tell me to my face that I can't even compete with a girl as young as Ellen! Am I really so undesirable?"

"Oh, Charlotte! I am so very sorry. I really thought Lieutenant Taylor was a good man." She tried to put her arms around me to console me.

"He probably is." I shrugged away. "I knew when he did not return for the autumn ball that he no longer wanted me. He has no reason not to pay his respects to Ellen Barlow. I'm the problem." I sat down hard on the chair by the fire in my bedroom. "I can't blame him for falling for someone else. I know I am not a prize of a woman, and I have no dowry to make up for it."

"Don't say things like that!" Mary Ann kneeled beside me. "No man could be worthy of you! You are so smart and so beautiful, and sweet too. I hope to be just like you some day. Don't worry! Your time for marriage will come soon."

I sighed as I let her wrap her arms around me. "I want to believe you. I really do, but I can't help but think he was my last hope for an advantageous marriage. I suppose all I can do now is wait even longer."

Chapter 5

The next couple of weeks passed slowly. Mr. Kingsley was still away on my father's business, and with the cold weather worsening, visiting with neighbors was rarely an agreeable option. I was sitting in one of the high-backed armchairs in my father's library, spending the afternoon reading yet another book of cures for various ailments, when I caught my thoughts drifting towards Eric. I was surprised to find myself almost missing his presence in the house. I shook it quickly off, chalking it up to the boredom that comes with the winter season. I had to admit that though time with him was rarely pleasurable, it was never dull.

No sooner had I removed him from my mind than he entered the room, to my astonishment.

"Mr. Kingsley," I greeted him and tried to gather my wits. "Miss Devonshire, I thought I might find you here."

I looked at him only briefly and nodded before returning to my book. I was determined to fight my inkling of desire for the company of this loathsome man. Not to be put off so easily, he crossed the room and sat in the armchair opposite me in front of the window. He leaned back and put his feet up. Really, was he still without any sense of decorum?

"So, what is the latest ailment you have learned to cure from your medical books?" he asked.

IN THE WAITING

I gave a little laugh. It struck me as funny that a man was asking me this when most men wouldn't like to hear that I was reading such books, let alone like to hear what I was learning from them.

"Last night I read a chapter on broken arms." I decided to play along with his game of taking my interest seriously. "If you ever need a splint, I'm the one for the job." I sat tall and made the most pompous face I could before laughing lightly at the idea of actually using what I had learned.

"I'll keep that in mind," he said simply, but he smiled with twinkling gray eyes. He viewed me with a mischievous grin, "I have something to show you."

"Mr. Kingsley, I can't possibly imagine what you might have that would interest me," I replied, turning my attention back to the book in my lap.

"It is not something I have; it is something I have found outside." I gave no answer.

"It will only take a moment."

The book became riveting, or at least I pretended so. "Please, Miss Devonshire, what harm could it do?"

I could think of several things. The last thing I needed in my search for a husband was a tainted reputation for becoming entangled with a less than honorable man.

"Believe me, it will be worth it. You have nothing to fear," he persisted.

"Fine!" I finally replied. "I suppose I'll have no peace until I see whatever it is you wish to show me."

"Wonderful!" he said, jumping to his feet and offering his arm. "Follow me, Miss."

I stood and rolled my eyes but let him lead me rather hastily out. "Well at least let me get my coat," I said, turning to go upstairs.

"No, no." He spun me back around. "Your coat is here

by the door. I asked Maggie to lend it to me." So now he even took the liberty of removing my own clothes from my room. Somehow, I wasn't surprised.

He succeeded in getting me out the door, and I noticed icicles hanging from the roof. He proceeded to lead me down the back hill towards the orchards. I nearly slipped several times on the icy ground. Thankfully he kept my arm and saved me from hitting the ground each time.

I had no idea where we were going or why we had to get there so quickly, but I was becoming increasingly annoyed. "Mr. Kingsley, I must insist. Where are you taking me?"

"I rode through the grounds a bit before returning to the house from my trip, and I discovered a most wonderful thing."

I didn't bother to protest further as I was too busy watching the ground, trying to keep my feet under me. We crossed the small creek at the bottom of the hill, and soon after, Mr. Kingsley stopped. I raised my head expecting to view the familiar sea of bare apple trees. Instead, I gasped as I saw the boughs of every tree now glimmering in the light as though they had been covered in blankets of stars. This was a rare and magnificent sight indeed. I had only seen this sort of frozen rain one other time in the years since coming to Long Island. I stood in awe of the beauty before me. I moved to touch a shining branch, and it made the sound of wind chimes as my hand brushed across it. Any annoyance I had felt at being taken from the comfort of the warm house vanished like the clouds that had parted to make way for the brilliant sun that now shone on this place of wonder.

He continued several paces ahead, "Come, it is even better further in."

I stood still at the edge of the orchard. He seemed

confused as to why I was hesitating. "What's wrong? Don't you trust me?" He feigned injury to his pride, but I could tell he was not hurt by the idea that I in fact did not trust him. In fact, he seemed almost to enjoy it. "No," I replied with both reluctance and severity, "I don't think I can trust a man as forward as you have been."

He looked at me inquisitively.

My annoyance returned at that point. I didn't expect that I would have to spell it out. "I don't want to go out of sight of the house, unchaperoned, with a man who kisses a woman he just met." As much as I wanted to read his expression, I couldn't bring myself to look him in the face.

He leaned back as if to get a good look at me. "What are you talking about?" he asked incredulously.

"Miss Winters," I said sheepishly, "at the autumn dance. I saw you in the room with her alone. She… she had her arms…" I couldn't describe the scene with his eyes looking so deeply into mine, searching for what I meant by my accusation.

"I didn't kiss her," he cut in rather sternly. "She advanced and I refused. I guess at first she thought I was just putting it off as a gentleman but would comply if I was more comfortable, for she tried making small talk. But when she started complaining about the Patriots as being so selfish as to rebel against the Crown who gave them their livelihoods, I defended the people's right to protect their interests when they feel threatened by their government. That was when she slapped me. After that, I just turned and left the room."

"Why didn't you tell me this sooner?" I asked with more than a hint of embarrassment in my voice.

"Why should I have?" The calm with which he answered vexed me, "You said it was none of your business if I wanted to pay my respects to her or not. I am sure you were more distressed because of what people must have thought of you, not because of me spending a few moments with Miss Winters. Besides, what good would it have done if I had told you?"

"Well, it..." I searched for a reason other than the truth. I knew I could not admit that it was because I was hurt that he didn't satisfy my desire for attention as the object of envy. I didn't even want to admit that to myself. "I just would have liked to know."

"Well, then next time I've been alone with a beautiful woman, I'll report to you the details of exactly what happened." The corner of his mouth turned up with a grin.

I turned away so he wouldn't see me blush. I struggled to make sense of this new information. He may not have kissed Ada Winters, but he was still the uncouth gentleman, no, uncouth boy, I thought him to be. Though I was not about to change my opinion of Mr. Kingsley, I had to admit to myself that perhaps his character was not as easy to paint as I had thought. And what was this about defending the Patriots?

"We should return to the house. It's getting late." I shivered in the cold wind that had come up.

I was surprised as he offered me his arm and a smile that was almost warm enough to make me forget about the frigid air of the building winter. As I accepted his arm, I caught myself contemplating a fleeting wish that he had offered to warm me with more than just his smile. How ridiculous! I chided myself for thinking such a thing after having just decided that he was still unworthy of the title gentleman, especially since he did not appear to be a loyal subject to the Crown.

We walked for a while in silence. Mr. Kingsley seemed to be taking his time getting us back to the warmth of the house. It gave me time to think over what he had shared.

IN THE WAITING

"What did you mean when you said the people have the right to protect their interests when they feel threatened?"

He studied me as if deciding whether I could be trusted to hear what he had to say. I knew that discussing such topics was dangerous in places like Setauket, which was under total British control. If certain people heard us discussing such things, they might question my family's loyalty and start talking of running us out of town like they did to the man who lived in Penningcoll. Despite having trained myself to keep quiet on such matters, I was afraid my imagination would get the better of me if I was left to interpret what he meant by the phrase on my own. I would rather hear the truth than assume the worst: that he was not a Loyalist.

"Do you not think that is true?" he finally said.

I thought for a moment. I wanted to say an emphatic "no," but I couldn't honestly disagree. "Well, I suppose I am of the opinion that the government is not actually threatening these people. The rebels are just using that idea as an excuse for demanding more than the government can give."

"I see," he replied, and I could tell he did. Perhaps he was not as much of a Patriot sympathizer as I momentarily feared. Still, I wondered, what were his thoughts on the war? But that was not something to concern a lady. I had more important things to worry about now that the Lieutenant was apparently out of the picture.

Chapter 6

By the time we were back inside, it was time to dress for dinner, so I hurried to do so.

Mary Ann was waiting in my room.

"Charlotte! I've been looking everywhere for you! You'll never guess who has come for dinner!"

I started taking off my warm things and rang the bell for Maggie. "No, Mary Ann, I can't imagine who has come, so you might as well tell me."

"Lieutenant Taylor, of course! Well, aren't you pleased?"

My heart quickened and I sank into a chair. "Lawrence? Lawrence is here?" I couldn't believe it. He was done with me. I knew that for certain. If he thought he could come back and play with my emotions… but no, likely he was here to see my father, not me. Well, I would not give him the satisfaction of seeing how he had set me back in my pursuits. I would be strong, and I would not let my old feelings for the Lieutenant resurface. I promised myself I would do this.

"Well, what are you doing just standing there!" I exclaimed, looking at the time, "Help me get ready! I have only a few minutes and Lieutenant Taylor must see that he has not crushed me."

Maggie came through the door in a tizzy. "Oh, Miss! Why do you wait until the last moment all the time!

IN THE WAITING

Supper'll be called in twenty minutes, and you ain't ready to meet your man."

"Well then hurry up and help me! Mary Ann, please get my cream dress, and Maggie, please try to do something with my hair. And he is no longer my man!" We bustled around the room until time had run out. Mary Ann hurried downstairs, but I took one last look in the mirror.

My hair was done up in twists and braids and adorned with pearls. My dress flowed elegantly with lace trim around the hem and belled sleeves. Small satin bows ran down the front of my bodice and my best brooch was at the top of them. Maggie reached up and let a curl drop onto my shoulder. I was ready to impress an officer of his majesty, not to win him back, but to encourage his regret.

I rushed down to the drawing room where the rest were gathered, but I stopped at the door to take a deep breath before entering. I could hear the voices inside.

"Have you served in the army, sir?" Lawrence was inquiring of Eric.

"No, sir, I have not. I am not well suited to your army," he replied matter-of-factly, if not curtly.

"Well, I am sure you have other ways of developing a reputation among *your* class," the Lieutenant sounded as if he was speaking to a boy.

Father laughed almost nervously. "We all have our parts to play," he said good-naturedly.

That was the cue that then would probably be a good time to change the subject by going in. I reminded myself one more time of the promise I had made in my room, lifted my head high, and entered. The men turned to face me from where they stood by the mantle. My attention was on Lawrence. I had almost forgotten how handsome he was, and it greatly weakened my resolve.

He had raven hair and deep blue eyes. He was tall,

even taller than Mr. Kingsley, and broad-shouldered. He looked every bit a Lieutenant and carried himself as such.

He crossed the room quickly and gracefully so that before I knew it, he stood quite close and stooped to kiss my hand.

"Miss Devonshire, you look more radiant than ever." He gave me a smoldering look.

I felt a flutter move through me and heat rose to my cheeks. I almost broke my promise. "Thank you, Lieutenant. It is a pleasure to see you again."

He turned to take my arm and led me to a chair near my mother. I looked up at him and saw a semblance of pride in his face. I followed his gaze and realized Mr. Kingsley was watching me intently, with a rather stern countenance. I looked quickly away, feeling vulnerable, as if he was looking right through me.

Mother spoke up, helping relieve the awkwardness I felt.

"Charlotte, I have invited Lieutenant Taylor to spend the week here so he might celebrate Christmas with us."

"Yes, Charlotte, isn't it a wonderful surprise?" added my father. I could tell in his tone that Lawrence's arrival had been a surprise to him as well. Like Mr. Kingsley, Father seemed to be trying to ascertain my true feelings about the arrival of our guest, but I had no idea what they believed the answer to be. I did not know how I felt about it myself, especially knowing now that Lawrence had not come to see my father. But I had to answer somehow.

I smiled demurely and replied, "We are happy to have you, sir. I hope you have a pleasant visit."

"I have every intention of doing so." His smile was lighthearted, but his eyes held something deeper that I could not decipher.

"We will be attending a Christmas Eve Dinner at the

IN THE WAITING

assembly hall," Mother continued, "No doubt that will give you the opportunity to see everyone, Lieutenant." My mother appeared to be doing her utmost to make Lawrence feel welcome. She had always adored him, particularly as a potential son-in-law.

"I look forward to it! And if Miss Devonshire would do me the honor of being her escort, my Christmas wish would be granted." My mother beamed, but I turned pink. There was his smoldering look again.

"Thank you, kind sir. It would be my pleasure to accompany you." It was his turn to beam. Father only smiled softly, and Mr. Kingsley seemed almost apprehensive.

Mrs. Phillips came to tell us dinner was ready, and Lieutenant Taylor stepped in to lead me to the dining hall. Throughout the course of the meal, we heard the latest news of the war and all the happenings in New York from Lawrence.

"And so, you think our victory is assured?" asked my mother.

"Well, ma'am, the way I see it, even if it isn't yet, it will be soon, for there is no possible way the rabble, even with the help of the French, will be able to beat the side that is in the right." He chuckled righteously, and my mother joined in.

"But enough talk of the war and of my diversions," he said, after he had exhausted the topics. "I would like to hear about what has been happening here in Setauket and your diversions." He leaned toward me, grinning mischievously.

I blushed and stole a glance at Eric, who only seemed to focus more intently on cutting his meat.

୬

When we had finished eating, my father rose, and we

all followed him back to the drawing room. Lawrence was helping me to a seat and lowering himself beside me when my father spoke.

"Lieutenant, might I have a word with you in my study?"

"Of course, sir." Then he spoke softly to me, "I'll be right back," and grinned.

"That reminds me," began Mother, "Mary Ann, I have some preparations for Christmas I would like to speak with you about. Will you join me in the Parlor?"

And so before we even had time to get comfortable, Mr. Kingsley and I were left alone in the drawing room. Still he did not speak. He just sat across from me, staring into the fire.

"You have been awfully quiet this evening," I commented. "Is everything alright?" "Hmm? Oh, yes, everything is fine."

I didn't believe him, but I allowed the silence to continue. There seemed no point in trying to converse. Eventually, Mary Ann reentered, and the increasingly uncomfortable silence was broken.

"Mr. Kingsley, I beg your pardon, but Mother says that Father is asking for you in his study."

"Thank you, Miss Mary Ann," he replied, rising, "I shall go to him directly." He gave a slight bow to excuse himself from my presence and followed my sister from the room.

As they were leaving, the Lieutenant came in. I looked past him to see Eric glance back over his shoulder from the doorway with a look of distrust. I could tell it was going to be a difficult week with both of these men under the same roof.

"Miss Devonshire." My attention turned back to the man in front of me. "I have missed you dearly these past months." He sat beside me on the settee, leaving adequate space between us to keep me at ease.

"We missed you too, Lieutenant Taylor." I looked down at my hands placed neatly on my lap and my cheeks flushed with heat.

"We? I had hoped you in particular would have felt at least a little of the pain I had from the distance between us." Now it was his turn to look down.

"Oh, why yes, of course!" I turned to look at him, "I only meant, well, I did not wish to seem…" I didn't quite know how to broach the subject of whether he expected me to miss him as a friend or as something more.

"If you are unsure of my feelings or intentions toward you, let me make them clear now." He slid closer to me and reached for my hand, but I pulled it away and turned to look out the windows at the white world beyond them.

"What's wrong?" he asked, moving still closer so I could feel his breath on the back of my neck. I didn't move.

I tried to sound cheerful in my response, "How is Miss Ellen Barlow? I heard you served her well in New York."

"Is that what this is about? Really, Miss Devonshire, I am surprised at you. Miss Barlow is a sweet girl, but I swear I only gave her my attention out of respect for her father's request that I keep an eye on her while she was there with only her aunt to tend her." Then he lowered his voice, and I felt him lean nearer my ear. "You are the only one I have eyes for, Charlotte."

I slowly turned to search his face for signs of teasing or jest, for he could not have meant what he said. When I had, I not only found sincerity in his eyes, but also, I found his face quite close to mine. The familiarity with which he spoke my name unnerved me. I could not move back because the arm of the settee was already pressing against my back. I couldn't believe it. He had actually meant what he said. He had not run away like the others. There was still hope.

I could have stood, but I found myself frozen and breathless before the handsome man so near me who had just made these declarations. He reached a hand to my cheek to tuck a loose strand of hair behind my ear, and I felt as if I could melt.

A loud bang of a shutter against the outside wall awoke me from the trance and I remembered myself. Pulling away, I rose, looking towards the windows again.

"Oh, such weather we are having. I do love a white Christmas though, don't you, Lieutenant?" He hadn't moved from his seat, but he was watching me closely.

"Please, call me Lawrence. Yes, I confess I do, particularly with someone as lovely as you with whom to share it."

My heart quickened. "And how do you find Mr. Kingsley? I hope you will not think the house too crowded during your stay," I said with a smile over my shoulder, trying to change the subject. Our closeness a moment before had made me uneasy, though I don't know why, since I had hoped for a romantic moment like that many times.

"I like him well enough, I suppose," he answered. "He does not seem to support the cause we fight for as passionately as he ought, though. I caution you to be wary of him." He stood. "I do not wish to see you hurt by an unscrupulous man."

I appreciated the sincere concern in his voice and faced him so I might give him a smile to show my thanks.

I could think of no way to continue the conversation, so after a moment of heavy silence I commented on the time and started to excuse myself.

"Wait," he said, and I turned back to him. "Dear

IN THE WAITING

Charlotte, if I may be so bold as to ask, may I escort you to your room?"

I hesitated but chose to accept his offered arm, and we made our way upstairs. I thought he was moving particularly slowly. He paused outside my door, holding onto my hand to keep me from going in.

"I have very much enjoyed your company this evening, Miss Devonshire, and hope I may have the pleasure often in the coming days." He stooped and kissed my hand ever so gently. I didn't know what to say, so I just watched as he continued down the hall to his own chambers.

∽

I closed the door behind me and leaned against it, letting out a deep, wistful sigh.

Lawrence *could* be mine again. After I had thought him gone, he had returned. Hope filled me. It did trouble me though, the tension between him and Mr. Kingsley. It would not be easy to be a proper hostess to them both if they opposed each other. I did not worry too much over Lawerence's warning of Mr. Kingsley, however, as I was sure my father would not hire an untrustworthy or dangerous man. Though he perhaps was not a man to become too close to, he was likely rather harmless, especially as I now knew what had actually happened with Miss Winters. And so, I felt no regret in developing a civil acquaintance with him. More than that, however, I would be fine to do without.

I had planned on reading the next chapter of my book, which was on heart sickness, but my own heart was too busy sorting out my emotions and dreams to focus on anything else. Hope had returned with the Lieutenant, and I had my work cut out for me if I was to secure him.

Chapter 7

When I awoke the next morning, it was far too cold and wet to walk far from the house, so I resigned myself to only visiting the widow's walk. To my surprise, as I lighted the last stair, the back of Mr. Kingsley's coat came into view.

"Mr. Kingsley, I didn't expect to find anyone up here."

"Nor did I," he answered, turning to face me in surprise. "You really shouldn't be up here, it being so cold and slippery."

"I could say the same to you, but I doubt it would make any more difference to you than your saying it to me." I grinned mischievously.

He laughed. "I see. Well then, I must at least ask that you be careful." "You have my word," I promised in mock sincerity, and laughed at myself.

For some time, we stood in the same silence from the night before, looking over the bay.

It seemed strange to me how at certain times Mr. Kingsley looked as if he carried a burden almost too heavy for him even though his character seemed to tend toward optimism and lightheartedness. Perhaps the war was taking more of a toll on this young man than it had on sturdy army men like Lieutenant Taylor. Though I did not know much of war, I had heard rumblings and rumors of men turned mad by its horrors.

IN THE WAITING

"I'm leaving for Fairfield." Eric broke the silence but continued to watch the water in the distance.

"You're going to Connecticut? When? After Christmas?"

"Now. The carriage is waiting to take me to the harbor as we speak." Then what was he doing up here, I wondered.

"Oh." I couldn't think of what I was supposed to say. At least I wouldn't have to worry about keeping the peace between him and Lawrence for a while. "May I ask you a question?"

"Of course," he said, but he sounded distracted by whatever he seemed to be watching or looking for.

"Why do you not like Lieutenant Taylor?"

He chuckled. "Shouldn't you first be asking *if* I like Lieutenant Taylor?" "Okay, *do* you like the Lieutenant?"

"No."

Mr. Kingsley was being as exasperating as usual. "Then why?"

"He is shallow and arrogant."

"Well, that is rather uncharitable of you! You have only known him for a day." "You did ask. I am only being honest."

I was vexed, but I had asked for it, so I ceased my protests. I felt quite disappointed in his admission. I don't know why I cared so much about what Mr. Kingsley thought of the man I hoped to marry. This was yet another case of me realizing how accurate Eric's first assessment of me was, and yet again, I did not like it.

"What are you even doing up here if you are supposed to be leaving?"

"Just thinking and watching, but now I must go." He suddenly seemed in quite a haste. "I bid you a good day, Miss Devonshire."

"Good day," I answered and watched him descend the stairs nimbly. He was quite a puzzle.

※

"I had something I needed him to take care of, but don't worry, he will be back by Christmas," said Father at breakfast. "I feel we should treat him as we would a son this Christmas. With his parents away, I am sure he would appreciate a family Christmas, don't you?" He looked inquisitively at my mother.

"Quite, I am sure." She smiled, but I could tell she was not thrilled that Mr. Kingsley seemed to be becoming a more permanent guest in our home than she had first anticipated.

"Lieutenant," she said, changing the subject, "I hope you will join us at church this morning, will you not?"

"Of course, ma'am, I would be happy to. I am of the opinion that we all need a day to appreciate and enjoy the blessings we have." He looked at me softly, and I dropped my face to hide my blush.

When we had finished the meal, we made preparations to be off and loaded into the carriage to go to service. Lawrence sat beside me on the way to and from the church. Between him and Mother, the conversation rarely paused for any significant length of time on either journey. My father, however, was quieter than usual. When I searched his face for what might be wrong, I could find nothing but what seemed to be a heavy worry. I decided I would ask him about it later.

While at the church, I had the pleasure of a sweet conversation with Mrs. Barlow. She, unlike her daughter-in-law, did not care about the imbalance in our families' ranks and treated me as amiably as anyone could wish.

"My dear Miss Devonshire," she had called, as she

navigated the crowd to come to me. "How are you doing today?"

"Hello, Mrs. Barlow! I am doing well. How are you?"

"Oh, I'm already ready for this cold to pass," she laughed a little and shivered.

I smiled, thankful for this simple and positive attention given without expectation.

☙

After we had arrived back home and had a light meal, I retired to my room for some quiet rest. Not long after I had settled myself in my soft chair by the fireplace with a warm blanket, I finished the book I had been reading, so I rose to go down to the library to fetch another.

As usual for a Sunday afternoon, the house was quiet, and I could hear the wind whistling outside as I headed downstairs. When I paused outside the library, I heard Lawrence and my father talking inside. I entered quietly, and since the room was large and dark, the gentlemen did not seem to notice me. I did not want to interrupt, so I quickly moved to find the next book in my father's collection on medical research.

"We are sending a large group down to Savannah, Georgia," Lawrence was saying, as if he was giving away a secret, though I was trying not to eavesdrop. "Among them are several New York Loyalists that I count among my acquaintances." He spoke with pride.

"I see," my father said, trying to sound impressed. "And what do they plan to do?" "Well, naturally we hope to successfully invade and occupy the city," he answered, annoyed that his indirect approach appeared not to have been clear enough. "I see. Well, that will certainly be a win for the British, eh?"

I turned from my shadow beneath the corner bookshelf

to look at my father. Though he at first glance appeared to be joyful at the news, the light from the candle between the men revealed the same worried expression I had seen on the carriage earlier.

Then, in my reverie, I dropped the book I was holding, and my presence was revealed. I bent quickly to pick it up, but by the time I rose again, both men were standing over me.

"Charlotte, you know better than to listen in on other people's conversations," my father scolded lightly.

"Yes, Father, I am terribly sorry. I didn't want to interrupt, but I came to find a book." "Don't worry, Mr. Devonshire, no harm is done," assured the Lieutenant before addressing me. "No doubt you wonder whether this will mean I will have to leave you. But do not fret, this move means they will not need me in New York for some time. I am now to be stationed in Setauket. There have been rumors of a spy ring hereabouts, and I have been tasked with uncovering it." He must have seen the concern in my eyes and mistaken it as being there for him since he continued, "I will be perfectly safe, I promise. And this will allow me to call more often, even after I move to town following my stay here—if your father does not oppose, that is?" He looked inquiringly at my father.

"I do not object if Charlotte does not." Now it was my father's turn to look at me with questions.

"I always enjoy the pleasure of your company," I replied after a nervous hesitation, and blushed. I didn't understand why I had such trouble encouraging this man's pursuit of me when I could not point to a single flaw in him.

I collected my new book, curtsied, and excused myself, heading back to my chambers. Lawrence was right to think I was concerned at his news but was mistaken

IN THE WAITING

as to the object of that concern. I knew what this course of action by our British troop would mean for so many innocent lives caught in the crossfire. I wished there was something I could do for them. The worry and weight I had seen on my father's face and on Mr. Kingsley's was no doubt nothing compared to what so many were facing on the mainland. I knew it was not my place to try to help in such matters, and I knew there was nothing I could do even if I did feel it was my place. But still, a part of me, a very small, deeply buried part of me, wanted to do more than chase a husband when so many were facing real suffering.

The next day, Mary Ann and I received a note from Fencomb inviting us to go into town with Ellen and Sarah Barlow to do some Christmas shopping.

"They say they will come in an hour with the coach to take us into Setauket, Mary Ann.

Do try and be ready in time. You know how Sarah hates to be kept waiting."

As fitting with Sarah's nature, the pair arrived much earlier than expected, but we were ready and eager to spend the small sum we had saved for our purchasing of gifts. Of course, Mary Ann had not planned ahead, so her sum was much smaller than mine, but she was just as eager to spend it. The Barlows, in contrast, appeared to have no spending limit.

"The reward for being born to, and then marrying, a wealthy gentleman," commented Sarah as she directed the placement of several large boxes onto the top of the carriage following a lengthy visit in a large shop. She said it as if she considered both to be her greatest achievements.

It was hard for me to believe how close we had once

been. Since Sarah had married, she had begun to put on airs and to treat me as a child, despite my seniority.

"Tell me, dear," Sarah began. Her eyes were on the spools of ribbons she was fingering in the next shop, but her tone suggested her full focus was on what she was trying to learn. "Do you and Lieutenant Taylor have an understanding?"

"Well, I… no, not officially, but…"

"You must secure him as soon as you are able, Charlotte," she interrupted. "You are not getting younger, dearest, and husbands do not grow on trees. Count yourself lucky, for it appears the Lieutenant will love you in spite of your less-than-ideal circumstances, but do not take it for granted!"

"Thank you for your concern, Sarah. I shall keep in mind your advice." Sarah was the kind of woman my mother no doubt wished I was, and I had struggled not to wish so myself. She seemed to have everything for which I was waiting.

"Ellen, you spent time in society with the Lieutenant in New York, isn't that so?" chimed Mary Ann. "What do you think? How soon, do you expect, shall we be hearing wedding bells?"

Ellen paused as if recalling significant events before replying, "I think Lieutenant Taylor is the kind of man who will not hesitate to bestow his affection and declarations of love on a woman he admires."

I didn't care for the somewhat knowing way in which she spoke her prediction.

"But I suppose a war can distract a man or delay his revealing what he otherwise would have shown much sooner." Mary Ann was trying to help; she obviously had hoped Ellen would say something that would calm my worries about Lawrence not having said anything official

IN THE WAITING

yet.

"Speaking of the war," put in Lady Barlow, "Edward is saying that we are quite close to winning. There have been rumors of spies in the area, but my Edward will track them down." She looked proud, as if she were responsible for her husband's contributions.

"Oh, good!" chimed Ellen. "Perhaps then all the officers will not be so preoccupied with war and can give the ladies some attention." She smiled demurely, then began giggling, and Mary Ann joined in.

They looked ridiculous, tittering in the middle of the shop. They began to leave, and Sarah and I followed. Mary Ann stopped abruptly just outside the door and spun around.

"Look, Charlotte! It's Lieutenant Taylor, across the street!" "What is he doing?" asked Ellen.

"Why, he has just come out of the jewelry shop!" Sarah exclaimed, and all six eyes looked at me. I blushed deeply.

"He could be in there for any number of reasons," I said. "This does not mean anything." "No, dear." Sarah put her arm in mine, and we started our walk home. "But this does give reason to hope," she concluded and smiled sweetly. I did not know if I had the patience to wait to find out.

Chapter 8

The next few days felt like a dream. Lawrence gave me every attention. We sat talking in the library for several hours on multiple occasions, and whenever I was in his presence I felt as if I were royalty. Time flew so quickly I was surprised to awake one morning to hear Maggie say, "Happy Christmas Eve to you, Miss. And a right wonderful day 'twill be I'm sure, for that Lieutenant be takin' you to the grand dinner at the assembly hall tonight."

"Can it really be Christmas Eve already?" I asked in disbelief, rubbing the sleep from my eyes as Maggie let the blinding sunlight come streaming through the window. "What time is it?" Normally I awoke before the sun rose.

"'Tis nigh on 11 o'clock, miss."

"Maggie!" I exclaimed, jumping out of bed. "Why didn't you wake me?"

"Don't fret, miss. Your mother told me to let you sleep as long as you would since you'll be having a late night tonight, and she wanted you to have your beauty rest."

"Oh." I sat down hard on a chair, trying to recover from the rush of standing so quickly. "I suppose that is for the best. I did stay up later than usual reading," I added sheepishly. I was not proud of my interest in medicine, knowing it was unbecoming to a lady, but I couldn't help myself. There was something wondrous about the ability to heal and restore life that made the universe seem less dark. Knowing what could be done to reverse the cruel hand of fate gave me hope in the midst of a breaking world. I found reassurance in my Christian faith as well, but to see the means through which God brought restoration was inspiring.

Maggie had set a cup of warm chocolate and some toast and jam on the small table by the fire, and I helped myself to the delights. There was a small rap on my door, but before I could answer, Mary Ann poked her head in. Upon seeing me awake, she lost her caution and burst into the room.

"Oh, good! You're finally awake! Look out your window!" She nearly dragged me from my chair to the sill, and it was worth it. We had only had small flurries and, of course, the one night of freezing rain, but now... now the world was covered in a heavy, white, shimmering blanket. I let out a breath of amazement.

"Now we will have to use the sleigh tonight! Oh, isn't it exciting? Father says I can go, since there won't be dancing, though I don't know why I shouldn't go even if there were, and we will get to use the sleigh!"

Though not as verbally expressive as Mary Ann, I was also very excited. There was something terribly romantic about a sleigh ride at Christmas. I imagined Lawrence tucking a warm blanket around my shoulders, sitting next to me on the way home... but then I remembered we would be with my parents, Mary Ann, and... Mr. Kingsley. I cringed. Maybe he wouldn't be home in time like he had planned. Or maybe Father would suggest he take his horse instead. But I knew Mother would more likely suggest such than Father. Oh well, there was nothing I could do about it now except prepare myself for the likely event of an awkward evening caught between two men who each seemed to feel he was more a part of the family than the other.

I did not have a chance to speak to Lawrence prior to our leaving for the evening because my mother insisted that my tea be brought to my room so as to give Maggie more time to dress me. I chose a forest green taffeta gown with gold embroidery and ribbons because I knew it would complement Lawrence's red uniform well. Maggie brushed my hair until it shone, then pinned it into place. The finishing touch was a simple gold necklace my father had given me back in England.

"You look mighty fine, Miss!" exclaimed Maggie as she studied her work. "That Lieutenant is a lucky man, if you ask me."

"Thank you, Maggie." I did look rather beautiful, compared to usual at least. Lawrence was waiting for me at the top of the stairs.

"Charlotte! You look absolutely ravishing!" He bent to gingerly kiss my hand.

I blushed hotly. "Thank you, Lieutenant. You look quite handsome." And he did. Usually, a uniform draws attention away from the man himself to make him more attractive, but with Lawrence, his uniform suited him so well it became like an extension of himself, highlighting his greatest features.

He led me downstairs where the rest of our party were waiting. "What a charming couple you make!" commented Mother.

"Thank you, Mrs. Devonshire, I am inclined to agree," Lawrence replied, and I blushed again.

As we waited for the sleigh, I surveyed Mr. Kingsley, who had not said anything and who seemed almost to be avoiding looking at me. His brown hair was neatly combed and tied, and he was wearing a navy suit with brass

IN THE WAITING

buttons and a crisp white cravat, and he held a dashing three cornered hat. Underneath, he was wearing a velvet vest...of the same color as my dress! I was dismayed! Everyone would think I had dressed so intentionally and that he was my escort! I was already embarrassed and wished I had time to change, but Thomas was announcing that the sleigh was ready.

Mr. Kingsley helped Mary Ann into the sleigh first, but when he turned to help me, he leaned forward, smiled, and whispered, "Don't worry, you wear the color much better than I."

I wanted to be annoyed with him for taking such liberties again, but I could not help but appreciate the effort he was making to help me feel less uncomfortable, so I smiled back and nodded slightly in silent gratitude. At least he seemed to have stopped enjoying my embarrassment.

I was thankful that Lawrence sat beside me, but Mr. Kingsley sat across from me, so, unfortunately, everytime we turned a corner, our knees would touch. This was not at all the romantic ride with the Lieutenant that I had been hoping for.

☙

The assembly hall was filled with gentry from all over the area, including many officers in his majesty's army. Among the guests were the Barlows, of course, and Miss Ada Winters.

Before the meal was served, hot tea and drinks were offered, and we were given the chance to mingle. I tried not to make eye contact with Ada, for if I did, I knew I would be forced to speak with her. Unfortunately, she would not be ignored. At her first opportunity, she joined me where I stood with Lawrence and Mr. Kingsley.

"How do you do, Miss Devonshire, Mr. Kingsley,

Lieutenant Taylor?" She had addressed all of us, but her eyes were fixed on Lawrence.

"Merry Christmas, Ada," I said, hoping to distract her.

"Indeed, Charlotte. No doubt this will be a much better Christmas for you than two years ago," she laughed with a terrible cackle. "Gentlemen, have you heard about what happened to our Miss Devonshire? Why, two years ago, a Mr. Lark, who had been calling her regularly, just up and left the island without so much as a goodbye! And that was just a few days before Christmas! People said it was because Charlotte did not suit him, that she was too heady and did not have the makings of a good wife, but I am sure there was more to it than that. Isn't that right, Charlotte?"

I had never been more angry with Ada than I was at that moment, and I had been angry with her many times. How dare she say such things… and in public, too!

"Miss Winters, I don't think…" Eric began.

"Oh, I am sure that was not the case, Miss Winters," interrupted Lawrence. "Perhaps he prefers brunettes and could not see past her blond hair." Then he and Ada shared a good laugh.

I felt as if I could cry, and I tried to free my arm from Lawrence's hold.

"Whatever is the matter, Miss Devonshire?" he asked. "Surely you cannot still be upset by an event of so long ago. Where is your sense of humor?" He and Ada continued to enjoy the moment at my expense.

I looked at Eric and was surprised to see pain and concern in his soft gray eyes, and he held my gaze for a moment, but Ada continued.

"And Mr. Smith! Oh, that is a good story too!"

"Why, Miss Winters!" Eric interrupted. "You look quite cold. Allow me to find you a place near the fire."

IN THE WAITING

Before she could object, he had her arm and was leading her away. I was more grateful to Mr. Kingsley than I could express in the silent exchange we had.

"Charlotte." Lawrence turned and spoke to me in seriousness, "You mustn't let such stories offend you so. Such things are behind you. After all, you have me now, and you are perfectly suited to me." He kissed my hand and stepped closer. He was right. I was wanted now, and that was all that mattered. A *Lieutenant* was assuring me of this! I almost forgot my previous embarrassment and anger, and I held my head high as we entered the dining room for the meal.

I did not have a chance to thank Mr. Kingsley that evening. He sat next to Ada at dinner, too far away for me to say anything to him in private. He did not appear to be enjoying himself, and I noticed him looking at Lawrence several times as if trying to read his movements.

Lieutenant Taylor, on the other hand, seemed to be enjoying himself very much. He whispered to me throughout the meal, making me blush with his remarks on my beauty and grace. If I were not so concerned with what everyone else was thinking, especially Mr. Kingsley who seemed particularly interested, I would have enjoyed myself just as much.

By the time we had returned home, we were all thoroughly exhausted, and Father suggested that it would be best if we all retired for the night. I noticed he looked rather carewarn for it being Christmas Eve.

"Good night, everyone! I shall see you all for Christmas breakfast in the morning." Lawrence started to take me upstairs. "Charlotte," Father continued, "may I see you for a moment?"

Lawrence released my arm and softly bid me goodnight before ascending with the others. "Yes, Father?" I joined him on a seat in the foyer.

"Charlotte..." He hesitated. "Are you... unhappy? That is, do the Lieutenant's attentions disturb you?"

"Why no, Father, I believe he cares for me. I very much appreciate his attention." I was confused as to why he was asking me such things. "Is something wrong, Father?"

He reached for my hand and smiled, but the shadow I had seen before was still there. "No, dear, I just don't want to see you hurt again... and I would hate to think I had allowed it to happen by having him in this house if his presence made you uncomfortable." He paused. "But if it does not, then I have no reason to ask him to leave." He stood and raised me to my feet. "Good night, darling, and merry Christmas."

"Merry Christmas. Sleep well." I kissed him lightly on the cheek and headed to my room.

As I undressed and made ready for bed, I contemplated the evening and came to two conclusions. First, Lawrence appreciated me. The hope and satisfaction that fact gave me was beyond words. I so desperately wanted to be loved, not only by a husband, but by my parents for having secured a husband who would ensure the future of my mother, my sister, and myself.

Having a husband meant being accepted as a woman of society rather than being seen as an old maid. Second, I concluded that though he was by no means a gentleman in many senses of the word, Mr. Eric Kingsley was honorable enough for me to consider him worthy of friendship. I no longer needed to feel guilty for any enjoyment I had in becoming more closely acquainted with him. This decision brought me more relief than I anticipated, and I looked forward to the morning with a lightheartedness I had not felt for some time. My only wish was that Father would feel the same way. He just needed to see that I cared

IN THE WAITING

for Lawrence as much as he cared for me and as much as Mother hoped I did.

Chapter 9

I awoke early on Christmas morning. I was so excited for the day and still had such joy from the night before that though the sun was barely rising, I could not fall back asleep. I decided I would go down to the library and enjoy the fire and the view from my favorite window chair of the white world outside. So, I dressed quickly, putting on a comfortable but appropriate dress for the household festivities of the day, grabbed my latest book, and quietly made my way downstairs.

The fire had just been lit and was burning gloriously in the large fireplace. After I had shaken the cold, watching the flames engulf the log, I went and stood in the alcove to observe the cardinals playing in the snow. When several minutes had passed, I heard the voice of Mr.

Kingsley in the doorway.

"Ah, Miss Devonshire, I did not think anyone would be in here." He started to go.

"No, please stay," I said quickly. He hesitated, then entered, but left the door open behind him. I waited until he had crossed the room and stood looking out the window beside me, though not very near.

"I wanted to thank you for what you did last night… taking Miss Winters away."

"Of course." He cleared his throat quietly. "I am sorry I did not do so sooner." He started to reach into his coat

IN THE WAITING

pocket.

"I would have expected you to tell me not to let it bother me so much. You said I cared too much what other people thought of me."

He quickly pulled his hand out and turned to look at me. "I do think you should not let what other people think guide you as much as it does, but there is no excuse for what Miss Winters did to you, and you had every reason to be upset by it. Just do not let her words rob you of your joy, or convince you that you deserved the treatment of your past suitors."

I noticed a twinge of something like anger in his last phrase, and I turned to face him. I felt more at ease looking into his kind, gray eyes now than I ever had before. His firm jaw and wavy hair had a familiar and comfortable air, and I suddenly felt that in some way, he was beginning to understand me, just as I was beginning to understand him. I sat down on one of the chairs between us and gestured for him to do the same.

"Mr. Kingsley, I am afraid I must have appeared quite vain and proud that first night we spoke. I admit I do care deeply how others see me. And I admit I should not care as much as I do about what people like Miss Winters, in particular, think of me, but I cannot help but desire the good opinion of certain other people."

"You mean like Lieutenant Taylor?" Eric's tone was soft, but his body became tense. I blushed. "Yes, and my parents, and other respected members of society."

"I cannot say what the Lieutenant thinks of you, and I do not know if I would care for the good opinion of some in the society here, but I do know that your Father at least thinks very highly of you."

"Thank you, but I am sure I am undeserving of his good opinion."

"Why is it that you spend your time craving the praise of others, but then when they give it, you say you do not deserve it?"

"I strive to deserve it," I corrected. "It is not that I blame others for not taking note of me.

I blame myself for not being noteworthy, and I see the clock ticking away the time I have to achieve what I must."

"And what is it you must achieve to be satisfied?"

I hesitated, then decided there was nothing to lose in confiding in him. He already didn't like me, and I doubted I could make the situation worse. He had already guessed as much in previous conversation. "Marriage," I answered, watching his face, "and perfecting my social skills to make my husband proud. Then everyone will have reason to accept me and think highly of me."

He did not say anything in reply, so we just sat, listening to the fire. "What about you? What must you achieve to be satisfied?"

"How do you know I am not already satisfied?" He grinned at me slyly.

I knew he was just teasing, but I chose to take him seriously. "Because I can see it in your eyes, in the way you walk, in the way you talk. You want more out of life than what has been offered to you thus far."

He looked surprised, then apprehensive. "You're right. Is it really that obvious?"

"No," I replied thoughtfully. "I think I've just seen more of you than most since you've come."

"Or perhaps you've been looking more than most?" He smiled slyly and I turned away in feign shock. Mr. Kingsley's remarks no longer surprised me as much as they once had.

Without looking back at him, I pointed out, "You still have not answered my question."

IN THE WAITING

He sighed. "I see the problems in the world, the pain, the suffering, the injustice, and I can't help but do something about it. I wish I could turn a blind eye to it, but I can't. I'm afraid it has made me rather cynical and rough." He laughed weakly then took a deep breath. "I do want more out of life, and I feel as though with every step I take forward, I am pushed even further back... and I see the same thing happening to so many innocent people."

"I understand. I believe that is why I am so interested in medicine. I like to know that there is hope for fixing at least some of the world's problems."

"And that is why I do what I do as well." He smiled kindly, as if he very much liked to find something we had in common.

"And what is it you do? Also, what did you mean when you said you would not care for the good opinion of some in the society here?" I asked, returning to his previous comment. Then I added with a nervous laugh, "I mean besides Miss Winters, of course."

He turned back to the view outside. "Well, if someone who has a worldview opposite of your own thinks well of you, then perhaps you are not living up to the standard to which you originally desired to hold yourself."

I thought for a moment about what he was saying. I did not even realize he had ignored my first question. "Do you disagree so completely with what our neighbors stand for?"

He looked at me and searched my eyes, though for what I could not tell. Then he answered simply and rather gravely, "Yes."

There was a knock at the door, which was still open, and my father stepped in. "Merry Christmas, you two! I've been looking for you! It is almost time for breakfast. Will you join us in the drawing room?"

We rose quickly, but I paused to look at Mr. Kingsley. We each smiled, and he gestured for me to go first. I somehow knew that our short conversation had marked the beginning of a more congenial and understanding friendship, and I had to admit it made me happy.

After we had all wished each other a merry Christmas and enjoyed a delicious breakfast, we made our way with smiles and laughter to the drawing room for the exchanging of a few small gifts.

From Mother and Father, I received a beautiful new blue day gown that would be perfect for spring weather.

"Oh!" I exclaimed when I had unwrapped the garment, "it's wonderful! Thank you, Father! Thank you, Mother!"

"You're welcome, dear," my mother replied. "Just because we cannot afford what we once could does not mean you have to walk around advertising that fact before you have a chance to marry."

I blushed and wished she had not said such a thing in front of our guests. I looked at Mr. Kingsley and I saw that the truth of what I had confided in him earlier that morning had become even more clear than it already was. The Lieutenant replied to the remark by giving me a laughing grin and a slight roll of his eyes. Mother should know to be more careful, but at least it did not seem to have mattered.

Thomas entered then and gave my father a letter. "This just arrived, Sir," he said. "Thank you, Thomas." We all watched intently as my father read the message with a grave look.

"What is it, darling?" Mother asked with a little panic in her voice.

IN THE WAITING

"Oh, it's nothing, dear, just some business news. Nothing to be concerned about. I do think I will have to go away for a few days, however." He paused and looked into the fire for a moment. "Would you mind if Mr. Kingsley and I stepped into my study for a few moments?"

"Of course," she answered, clearly confused as to what might concern her husband that she could not hear and Mr. Kingsley could. Nevertheless, she shrugged it off, likely reminding herself that business was not a woman's area of concern.

My father and Mr. Kingsley took their leave and with it the wind from the sails of our celebrations.

"Mary Ann," my mother broke the silence, "would you like to try your new music book?"

Mary Ann rose and followed my mother to the spinet across the room where she sat down to enjoy the book under the supervision of the one who had given it to her.

Lieutenant Taylor took his opportunity and asked, "Charlotte, would you do me the pleasure of accompanying me on a sleigh ride? I am afraid last night was not quite the romantic winter ride I had hoped it would be." He chuckled and I laughed timidly, keeping to myself the fact that I had also been disappointed about the crowded nature of our transportation.

"I would love to!"

"Wonderful! If you would get your coat, I will meet you in the foyer in ten minutes." He smiled with shining blue eyes.

༄

When I had bundled myself up and quickly checked my appearance, I hastily descended the stairs to where Lawrence was waiting.

"Come," he said, offering his arm and leading me

out the door, "a magical ride awaits us." He gestured to some mystical beauty in the air, and I followed his gaze in anticipation.

I was surprised to see that it was not my father's sleigh that we would be traveling in, but a hired sleigh with fur blankets on the seat and silver bells on the snow-white horses.

"Oh, Lawrence!" I exclaimed, "How beautiful it is!"

He beamed. "I knew you would like it." He helped me up and sat beside me before tucking one of the blankets around us.

We drove for some time in silence, just enjoying the view of snow-topped trees and the warmth of each other's presence in the midst of the cool wind.

"Charlotte?" Lawrence began softly so as not to disturb the wonder of the moment. "I have something for you." He reached into his coat pocket and pulled out a small box. Then he handed it to me.

I looked at him and marveled at the fact that I was being given a gift on a romantic sleigh ride with a handsome Lieutenant of class and wealth. Though I had been hoping for this, I could barely believe that it was actually happening.

"Open it," he urged.

Inside I found an ornate gold brooch with little emeralds and sapphires set in it. I gasped. I had never been given anything so fine. I found myself at a loss for words and simply sat there stroking the piece in pure awe.

"I hope it suits you," he continued, seemingly uncomfortable with the silence. "Oh, yes! It is absolutely wonderful!"

"Good," he sighed with relief. "I want everyone to see how much you matter to me and that I have the desire, and the means, to spoil you. Now that my uncle has passed, I finally have my rightful fortune."

I blushed. I liked the idea of being spoiled almost as much as I loved hearing that I truly mattered to Lawrence.

"May I?" he asked, gesturing to the brooch in my hand. "Please," I replied, as butterflies filled my stomach.

He removed his gloves and took the brooch. He slowly unclasped my coat to reveal the top of my dress and gingerly pinned the piece in place. His warm, deft hands slowly moved to caress my neck and shoulders, sending shivers through me. Was this what it felt like to be in love? He slid my coat back over me and fastened it again. I tried to catch my breath, but I felt as if I was on the edge of my seat, waiting to see what he would do next. He leaned toward me but then paused and leaned back, instead choosing to put his hand in mine.

"I know I was away for too long," he said, "so I wish to make up for lost time. As I said the other day, I will be able to call more often now that I am staying in Setauket. I promise, I will not run away as others have before me." His eyes were tilted down in a sincere, almost earnest expression.

I clasped his hand between mine, lifting it to my lips as I had seen Lady Barlow do with Sir Edward's, and I smiled my deep appreciation for his kind words. The look he gave in return assured me I had chosen well by showing such affection.

Chapter 10

Lieutenant Taylor did not disappoint. He came calling as often as he could without encouraging *too* much gossip. Every time he came over, my mother managed to give us at least a little time alone. If it were not for my father being out of town for those several days, he would have likely put a stop to her manipulation. However, as it were, I did not mind the seclusion as it gave us the opportunity to become more closely acquainted with each other much faster than if we were in the presence of others. There was occasionally minor discomfort on my part simply because I was not used to the intimate way in which he showed his affection. Still, affection was always welcome from him, and so, though our solitude at times gave me pause, I did my best to ignore my hesitations, believing them to be rooted in the fear of disappointing Lawrence with my awkwardness. Perhaps if I had been more accustomed to such advances, or believed more strongly that I was deserving of them, I could have responded with more encouragement, the way I knew high class ladies would.

One day, we were sitting in the front parlor together, having tea and talking. My mother had shut the door on her way out of the room as she had done multiple times before.

I was busy serving the tea when I noticed him staring at me strangely. "Why do you look at me like that?" I

IN THE WAITING

asked.

His eyes sparked and he grinned. "I was just thinking how wonderful it would be to have a wife like you to serve me like this every day."

I blushed with pleasure at this compliment.

He stood to receive the cup I offered, but instead of sitting back down in his chair, he joined me on the settee. We sipped our tea for a few moments before he continued.

"Charlotte," he began, setting his cup down, "how is it that I have won your favor?" "I should think that would be obvious," I replied.

"Humor me," his eyes pleaded, but his smile was soft and teasing.

"Well, you are a gentleman." I spoke timidly. "You're rather dashing in a uniform, and you love me…or, I mean…care for me like no man has before. My heart races in your presence." Heat rose to my face. I had never been so open with a man before, though I found I liked the rush it gave me.

Lawrence was beaming. He slid his hand into mine and said, "I *do* love you." My heart felt as if it could leap from my chest.

Just then, there was a loud knock at the door, and it was opened hastily by none other than Mr. Kingsley. He stopped short when he saw us. I was suddenly made aware of how bad it must look to find us the way we were. I stood quickly, but I could not free my hand from Lawrence's, for he held fast to it while he slowly rose.

"And what can we help you with?" Lawrence asked Mr. Kingsley, with a hint of annoyance in his voice.

Eric looked at our clasped hands and clenched his jaw. His eyes narrowed as they moved back to Lawrence's face. He seemed about to speak, but he shook his head slightly, then looked straight at me. "Miss Devonshire, I am in need of your assistance. Would you be so kind as to come with me?" His tone was even, but his face and eyes told me this was more than a lighthearted or needless request.

After my initial surprise had passed, I replied, "Of course. Forgive me, Lawrence, I must go." I succeeded in freeing my hand and hastily followed Mr. Kingsley from the room.

He did not pause for any explanation but hurried me to the back door where he helped me into my coat, which he had once again taken the liberty of fetching for me. He took me out into the cold and began walking quickly away from the house.

"What is it? Where are we going? What is happening?" I kept asking, and I struggled to keep up with his long strides as he led me down the back slope and through the orchards.

"You will see, just please hurry!" he replied again and again. The scene was reminiscent of our excursion not so long ago.

I was already tired from the last several days of entertaining the Lieutenant, and I had not slept well the night before from the excitement of it all, so this brisk walk was not particularly easy. At last, I looked up to see we were arriving at the abandoned house of Penningcoll that I had so often looked upon from the widow's walk.

"What are we doing *here*?" I wondered aloud. We climbed the steps, and Eric pushed open the heavy, rusted door to reveal a large, rather dirty room.

There were piles of furniture stacked in the corners, and spiderwebs and dust covered nearly everything. A small, dying fire gave only a little light to the room. and the windows were so dirty that there was barely any sunlight. Then I noticed that on the floor by the fire were two figures, no, three. There was a baby.

IN THE WAITING

As my eyes quickly adjusted, Eric took my arm and pulled me towards the group. I saw then that it was a young mother, who looked barely over 18, holding the baby. The other form was an older man who was lying down, unconscious, covered in a thin blanket.

"Please, miss, please help my father," the girl begged. "We cannot escape with him like this." She lifted the blanket to reveal a thoroughly bloodied leg with bits of dirty cloth clinging to it. I raised a hand to my mouth and gasped. I kneeled, knowing that I had the knowledge to help these poor people and yet just as aware of my inexperience in actually dealing with these sorts of things. It only took a moment to realize that the wound had been made by a gunshot, which could mean only one thing.

I stood quickly and crossed the room to where a small basin with water stood. Mr.

Kingsley followed me.

"These are runaway Patriots!" I exclaimed softly so only he could hear. "What would everyone think of me for helping the enemy? It would be like betraying my family! How could I do such a thing?"

His eyes were filled with desperation and entreated me to reconsider. I looked at the woman and her child huddling together in fear.

"How can you not?" Eric asked.

My head was spinning. Nothing was making sense. Why were these people in this house, and how did Mr. Kingsley know they were here? How involved with them was he? Why had he brought me here knowing that my family is loyal and that I would have severe qualms about helping Patriots? As torn as I felt, I knew I had no choice. I had to help this man and his family. At least, I had to try, for there was no guarantee I could succeed. They needed me, and it wouldn't be Christian to turn away.

I looked at Eric and conceded. "Do you have the necessary supplies?"

"I have water ready to boil and clean bandages and what tools I could find on the small table by the fire. I also took the liberty of borrowing a few books from your father's library." He removed the books from a small bag that I just now noticed he had carried with us from the house. How he had been so sure I would agree to help I did not know.

We both washed our hands in the basin, and I allowed myself a quick yawn before we set to work. The task was painstakingly slow, but with Mr. Kingsley's help, eventually all the cloth and dirt were removed from the area, and the wound was exposed. I could see the bullet still lodged in the man's shin and knew it had to come out. I reached for the small pair of pliers Mr. Kingsley had prepared and took a deep breath, but I couldn't stop my hand from shaking.

Eric looked at me warmly but seriously. "It is okay. You can do this. You must do this." He put his hand on mine, and I began to relax. Steadily, I pulled out the bullet.

With that done, I felt a little unsteady in my fatigue, but said, "It will need to be stitched."

He nodded and went to get the needle and thread. "Take all the time you need," he said as he handed them to me. It was tedious and time-consuming work, but I managed to complete the gruesome task. We both breathed a sigh of relief, as did the man's daughter, who had been watching all the while. Together, we finished washing the wound and wrapped the leg in clean bandages.

Mr. Kingsley rose, and I tried to do the same, but as I stood, I began to sway and feel quite dizzy. Just as I thought I was going to faint, a pair of strong arms caught me and carried me to a chair in the corner where they set

IN THE WAITING

me down carefully.

"Charlotte, Charlotte," a muffled voice called to me.

I began to awake and saw Mr. Kingsley kneeling in front of me, his hands clasping mine, trying to rub the warmth back into them. I realized it was he who had been calling me. That was the first I had ever heard him say my Christian name. I confess I liked the sound of it on his lips. I smiled and closed my eyes again. I was so tired and cold.

※

I woke to the sound of horses' hooves crunching the snow outside and realized I was lying on a bed of blankets on a wood floor. I raised my head, but a sharp headache caused me to quickly lay it back down. I then remembered what had transpired and realized I had no concept of how long I had been asleep. Heavy footsteps outside were followed by the opening of the door and Mr. Kingsley rushing in.

"She is awake and just fine," the voice of the young mother told him.

I opened my eyes and smiled weakly at him. "I am sorry. I hope I have not caused too much alarm."

Eric looked as if he was just as tired as I was. He smiled back at me but did not answer my remark. "I have brought a horse so that you needn't walk back home." He then moved to check on the man we had tried so desperately to save.

"Mr. Milton, Mr. Milton," he said, gently pressing on his shoulder. The man groaned in response.

"Bridgett? Bridgett, is that you?" he spoke groggily.

"I am here, Father." The girl rushed to the man's side, still closely clutching her infant.

"I believe he will be just fine," Eric told her. "I must get Miss Devonshire back home. It is already quite dark.

But I will be back early in the morning to resupply the water and food.

There should be enough firewood to last you through the night."

"Thank you, sir, and thank you, miss," she added, as Mr. Kingsley began slowly to raise me to my feet. "You have saved my father's life. How can I ever repay you?"

"There is no need," Mr. Kingsley answered, translating my weak smile. "Just stay out of sight and keep warm."

"We will. God bless you both."

And with that, Eric helped me outside and onto his horse. He led the animal back across the fields, through the orchards, and up the hill. It was later than I had expected. The procedure, and my subsequent, unplanned nap, must have taken hours. We had clearly missed the evening meal, so I wondered why the house seemed so quiet as Mr. Kingsley helped me inside. I would have expected everyone to be out looking for us.

Eric appeared to know what I was thinking because he offered the explanation I was looking for. "Before I came to ask for your help, I told Mrs. Phillips that if we were not back in time, she should tell your mother that you were not feeling up to dinner and that I was called away on business for the evening, both of which were true excuses, I might add."

I was rather impressed.

"Would you like me to help you to your room?" he offered.

"Thank you, but I'm sure I can manage," I replied, stepping in the direction of the staircase.

"Miss Devonshire?" he called softly.

I turned around, noticing he had returned to proper formality. For a man who could be so familiar and even brazen in conversation, he managed to adhere to social rules surprisingly well when needed.

"Thank you." His gratitude was simple, but sincere. "You're welcome."

We held each other's gaze for a moment, then he spun on his heel and went to care for his horse.

I was so tired and dizzy as I climbed the steps that I almost wished I had accepted Mr. Kingsley's offer, but I knew if anyone happened to see us, especially Lawrence, it could bring disaster.

I didn't bother to ring for Maggie, deciding it would be best if she didn't have the chance to ask all her questions. When I had thoroughly cleaned myself, I finally sank into bed and let sweet sleep overtake me.

Chapter 11

I did not see Mr. Kingsley for the next several days. I learned the morning after our secret dealings at Penningcoll that he had left on business a few hours before I woke. Father returned that day in much better spirits, though he was not especially happy to hear how much time the Lieutenant had spent at Longford. Thankfully, Lawrence had moved to a boarding house in town before Father had had a chance to ask him to leave himself. I suppose I was grateful for how protective he could be, and yet I was also glad that mother balanced his caution with her tendency to encourage socializing.

The new year was upon us, and with it came word that British forces had successfully invaded Savannah, Georgia on December 29th.

"Have you heard the tremendous news?" Lieutenant Taylor asked us all as he entered the Parlor one afternoon, for he still visited Longford whenever he had the chance.

"Yes, we have," my father replied without looking up from his book.

Mother and Mary Ann simply smiled and went back to their needlepoint, no doubt with the intention of encouraging Lawrence's attention to turn towards me.

Lawrence seemed disappointed that he did not raise a better response from the room. He came and sat in a chair next to mine, and I closed the book I had in my lap as he began to speak.

"This means the war is almost over! We can begin to think about life after the war!" He reached for my hand. It was then that my father finally gave the Lieutenant his attention.

Lawrence noticed the look of warning and stood. "Forgive me, I do not mean to be so loud, I am just proud of our country." I was sure he knew that his volume was not what had bothered Father.

Was this excitement for the future a hint at a proposal? The idea sent my heart racing.

Could I really be so close to catching what I had spent so many years chasing? Then my thoughts turned to my father. Would he be against the match? Hadn't he always wanted me to find a man who could take care of me and Mother and Mary Ann after he had gone? And yet, he seemed so particularly hard on Lawrence.

༄

When Mr. Kingsley arrived the next day, I took the first opportunity I had to ask him about the Miltons.

"Are Mr. Milton and Bridgett still at Penningcoll?" I whispered as we stood in the corner drawing room awaiting the noon meal. I was sure the others were out of earshot and preoccupied enough with their own conversation that I would be safe asking such a question.

"Yes," he answered hesitantly. "Well, can I go and see them?"

He raised his eyebrows and leaned his head back as if to get a better look at me. "You really want to go back? I thought you wanted as little to do with the situation as possible. You said it was like betraying your family."

I eased the enthusiasm of my approach and said, "It wouldn't be very compassionate of me to turn away from a family in desperate need, now, would it?" I didn't tell him that I was also simply curious to hear more about them and their story.

He grinned. "No, no it wouldn't." He continued to look at me with that half-cocked smile until I began to feel uncomfortable.

"Well?"

"Yes, sorry, let's see… If you go out riding after the meal at, say, one o'clock, I can meet you at the edge of the orchard and go with you the rest of the way."

Mrs. Phillips entered then and announced that the food was ready.

"I shall see you at one o'clock," I whispered. Then it hit me that I had just made secret plans to meet Mr. Kingsley, *alone*, and I had even whispered to him about it! I remembered just how shocked and upset I had been when Mr. Kingsley had behaved similarly the night we met, yet here I was doing the same thing. I had better be careful, not only for the Miltons' sake, but for my own. It was crucial that news of what Eric and I had done and were planning to do did not spread. Even if the subject of our meeting was not revealed, I would still have much to answer for.

☙

Nevertheless, at the appointed time, I met Mr. Kingsley at the edge of the orchard, or rather, just far enough inside so as to hide our meeting from the view of the house. I was glad Lawrence had no plans of visiting that day because it meant I had the entire afternoon free.

"Where is your horse?" I asked as he stood from where he was leaning against a tree, holding his coat tightly around his chest.

"I thought it would be suspicious if we both took one

from the stables."

"Well, you can't very well walk in this snow. We would freeze before we got there.

Come, get on."

I moved forward in the saddle. "Are you sure?" He hesitated.

I appreciated his reserve, another sign he was more of a gentleman than I had first thought. "Yes," I said with a tone that thanked him for asking. "Now hurry." Again, I couldn't really believe what I was doing, but my curiosity had won, and after all, it wasn't as if we were in public.

He mounted deftly, but thankfully kept his arms at his side rather than putting them around me as we rode. I was surprised that he seemed to have no difficulty in staying on, but then, he was an athletic sort of man, though not as strong as Lawrence, I was sure.

When we had traveled the mile or so to our destination, Mr. Kingsley helped me dismount. He knocked a special rhythm on the door before we entered.

"Oh, miss! You have come back!" the young mother exclaimed with a look of joy. "Yes." I smiled. "And please, let me formally introduce myself. My name is Miss Charlotte Devonshire."

"A pleasure to make your acquaintance, Miss Devonshire," she replied with a small curtsy. "My name is Bridgett Olsen, and this is my son, James Jr." She unfolded a corner of the baby's blanket so that I might see his face.

"Oh!" I exclaimed. "He's beautiful!" I felt keenly my own desire to have children, and I imagined, for a moment, the life I still waited for.

"He takes after his father." Bridgett smiled at her son, but she did not seem happy. "My husband is away," she began. "We have not seen him these many months." She paused and took a feeble breath. "He has yet to meet his son." She looked up, and I saw the glint of tears in her tired eyes.

Instinctively I stepped forward and embraced her and her son. "Oh, Bridgett." I couldn't explain it, but I was suddenly flooded with such deep compassion for this young mother. I shuddered to think of how close I was to turning my back on her and her family the day before, just because they were patriots. They were people who were hurting and needed my help, regardless of what side they were on.

I stood back and smiled at her, then turned to see that Mr. Kingsley was watching us with a smile of his own—and was that a tear I saw? But before I could be sure or interpret his strange look, he moved to stoke the fire.

"I want to thank you again, Miss Devonshire," Bridgett continued. "You saved my father's life."

I looked down at where the older man lay and noticed with some embarrassment that he was awake and had been watching us warmly the entire time.

"I would like to thank you as well," he said weakly, "and just as soon as I am well enough to travel, we will be out of your way. I know how much you are risking by letting us stay here."

I remembered then how little I knew about why the Miltons *were* here, and why and how Mr. Kingsley came to be involved with them. "Well, it is not our house," I replied, "so there is no way anything can be traced back to us unless we are caught in the act." Mr. Kingsley cleared his throat from his place at the fire, but I couldn't see his face. "And please, don't think anything of what I did. I couldn't very well refuse to help you just because of our difference in loyalties."

Mr. Milton and Bridgett exchanged a nervous look.

"You mean you are not a Patriot?" the man asked

hesitantly.

"Why no, of course not. My parents are Loyalists and I live amongst Loyalist high society. How could I be a Patriot?"

"Isn't believing what is right the only important thing?" Bridgett began carefully. "What does it matter if everyone around you thinks one way if it is not what is right?"

I was shocked at her frankness. It reminded me of many of the conversations I had had with Mr. Kingsley since his arrival at Longford. All eyes were on me, even Eric's. He had looked up from the flames, and it felt as if even the wind outside was waiting for my reply to this weighty question.

"Well, I… I suppose not." My answer surprised me. "But aren't the Loyalists in the right?

Didn't this whole mess start from colonists simply being selfish and rebellious?" "Do you know why my husband hasn't met his son yet?" continued Bridgett. I shook my head, beginning to feel the severity of the conversation building.

"Not long before we were married, my family escaped from our home only moments before it was burned to the ground by British troops moving through our small town. When my brother tried to stop them, he was shot and killed right in front of us. We ran for miles and miles until we reached a camp of General Washington's men. We were able to send word to my fiancé from there, and he joined us for only a few days, long enough for us to be married, before he offered to become a courier of spy messages for the General."

"Why would the British soldiers do such a thing?" My voice was barely above a whisper as I tried to process this information. "I have always thought the King's army to be noble."

"The group of officers demanded lodging in our home, and we refused," she explained matter-of-factly.

"They wanted more than that from my sweet girl," Mr. Milton added, "and my most adamant refusal to their desires pushed them over the edge."

I gasped. I couldn't believe I was hearing such things. "Surely they were dismissed immediately for their actions!"

"Miss Devonshire, I don't think you understand. These were the officers in charge. I count myself lucky. Many families were not able to escape as we have."

"Then why are you back on British-occupied land?" I asked.

"We are trying to make it to Connecticut, where my husband will soon be able to join us in the safety of Colonial-controlled Fairfield."

I sat down on a chair that had been pulled out from under the dust cover that was draped over most of the furniture.

Silence ensued for several minutes.

"I think you are in need of some more firewood if you are to stay warm for the couple of days it will take for us to get you on a whaling boat that can carry you across the sound," Mr.

Kingsley commented. "There are some logs outside. It shouldn't take long to chop you some. Miss Devonshire," he added, turning to me, "may I speak to you?" He gestured toward the door.

"Certainly." I would not mind a chance to breathe some fresh air and to think for a bit about what I had just heard.

"I'll heat some water, so we can have some of this coffee when you come back in, Miss Devonshire." Bridgett

IN THE WAITING

gestured to a crate of food and goods that Mr. Kingsley must have brought for them.

"Thank you, Bridgett, and you may call me Charlotte." She smiled, and I stepped past Mr. Kingsley into the cold. "May I?" he asked, when the door had closed behind us.

I looked at him with what must have been a very odd face as I was trying to decide if I should be annoyed at his presumption or flattered at his desire for familiarity.

"You can call me Eric," he offered, as if it was tempting bait, and picked up the ax.

I sat on the edge of the porch, letting my feet dangle, and thought for a moment. "Very well, but only when we are not in public." I raised my chin, but he grinned as if he had made a great step in the direction he wished to go.

What harm could it do here? It was not as if we were truly in the real world here anyway.

He lifted the blade above his head, and I was surprised at the ease with which he split a piece of wood in two. Then his smile began to wane, and he clenched his jaw as I had seen him do many times when he appeared to be contemplating a difficult question. "May I ask you something?"

"You've never waited for permission before." I smiled and raised an eyebrow. His face remained unchanged.

"Do you still think the side of the king is the right one to be on?"

I should have been shocked at the question, but after what I had just learned, I was asking myself a similar thing. I thought for some time, and Eric did not press me further, but instead kept chopping the wood.

"I don't know anymore."

He stopped mid-swing of his ax.

I continued. "I know you don't think so, though I don't know why it took me so long to see it. You haven't exactly hidden your opinions well." Eric came and sat by me, and we looked through the trees covered in snow that lay beyond the Penningcoll. "I suppose the way I see it, the people have a right to ask for some authority over their own lives. And if they are answered with atrocities such as what I just heard, I suppose they do have the right to defend themselves." I paused. "I cannot say that I am quite sure they have a right to cut themselves off from their government, even one that they believe abuses them," I added quietly. "My father, though loyal, has always taught us the importance of justice and of godly compassion. I see how these principles maybe ought to point me towards the Patriots."

Eric sighed, not in frustration or weariness, but in what sounded like relief. "You have no idea how glad I am to hear you say this. As you have said, I have struggled to keep my views to myself, and I have hoped that you would be able to understand and even agree with me. Though you do not yet agree in full, I have faith you soon will."

"Why would you care about what I thought of you? I thought you cared nothing about what other people thought of you." My question was sincere, not teasing or sarcastic.

"It is not that I wished you to think well of me, I knew that would be and will be impossible. I wished for your own sake that you could come to a conclusion of this importance on your own, apart from your family and friends."

"Well, I am not completely sure, though now I see more value to the other side than I ever have, thanks to you. I would, however, appreciate you not making my somewhat altered, or rather, discovered, views known to anyone. I would be ruined socially even if they only suspected I did not fully support the British. Oh! And I didn't even think of Lawrence. He can't know that such terrible things have happened, I'm sure! He is a noble gentleman, and I would not hurt him by letting him know of my sympathy towards the Patriot cause for anything."

Eric didn't look at me, and his eyes were narrow. "You have my word," he promised. "But just you wait, you will be a Patriot before you know it," and he grinned once again.

Chapter 12

The next afternoon, I sat in the parlor with a cup of tea, and my mother decided that it was the right time to interrogate me.

"Charlotte, dear, I would like you to be honest with me. Have you succeeded in making Lieutenant Taylor propose yet?"

"Mother!"

"What?"

"If he is going to propose, it will be his own choice."

"Well, he might need some extra encouragement to be persuaded to take you for a wife."

Her remark stung sharply. I knew I was not the most desirable of women, I did not need her to say it so frankly.

"Might I remind you that you are not getting any younger. This may be your last chance to secure a husband of any worth or consequence. As it is, the Lieutenant is not exactly wealthy."

"Thank you, Mother, until now I was completely unaware of my waning chances for a happy life."

She raised her eyebrows but did not respond.

"I'm sorry, Mother, I do not mean to be impertinent." I sighed and straightened my shoulders. "Lieutenant Taylor is a wonderful man, and if his actions these past weeks have been any indication, I do think there is good reason to believe he will propose." I smiled sheepishly.

IN THE WAITING

My thoughts had been so preoccupied with helping the Miltons and making sense of my uncovered opinions, that I had not thought about Lawrence for some time. Doing so now brought color to my cheeks.

"Good! Good," she replied as she sipped her tea. "He mentioned something to me the last time he was here about returning before the end of the week, so you may look forward to that."

There was a knock at the front door, and Thomas answered it.

"Now whoever could that be in this weather?" Mother commented, for a light snow had been falling most of the day.

I heard voices convey the typical pleasantries, then Thomas came into the parlor and announced our guest.

"Mr. Andrew Barlow, ma'am."

"Welcome, Mr. Barlow." Mother curtsied and I followed suit. "What brings you here while the weather is still so cold? I do hope no one is ill."

"Oh no, nothing like that. This is more of a business call than a social call. I am actually here to see Mr. Kingsley," he said, looking around the room nervously, "though seeing you ladies is a pleasant treat." He smiled and bowed slightly.

"I see," replied Mother, but it was clear that she still did not understand what reason he could have for visiting Eric. "I believe he is with Mr. Devonshire in his study."

"Thank you, ma'am." He bowed again and left the room. "Whatever could that have been about?" she wondered aloud.

"I'm sure I don't know, Mother. Perhaps he wanted to ask him some question of spirituality."

Not much happened in the following two days. I didn't have a chance to talk to Eric in private about the Miltons, and I decided it would probably be best anyway if I waited for him to broach the subject. The last thing I needed was for Mother, or anyone for that matter, to start worrying about my spending time with him, let alone discover what we had been up to or what my position was regarding the war.

I also found it rather hard to forget what I had learned from Bridgett when I received the expected call from Lieutenant Taylor. We sat by the fire in the drawing room that afternoon as Mary Ann played the spinet. Lawrence had asked me to read aloud, and so he listened most intently, or at least, he watched me most intently as I read from Shakespeare's *Julius Caesar*.

"'Liberty! Freedom! Tyranny is dead! Run hence, proclaim, cry it about the streets,'" I continued, then paused, though Lawrence did not seem to notice. "I suppose this must sound quite familiar to you?" I suggested, without looking him in the eye. I knew I needed to be careful with this topic, but I had to be sure where he stood.

"Hmm?" His mind appeared to have been wandering. "I'm sorry. Yes, I have heard some captured low-life patriots try to claim similar things."

"Lawrence, I know we are on the right side, but are you sure *all* that the British troops have done is completely necessary for the cause?"

"Of course we are on the right side!" He sat up straight and his cheeks were flushed. "And anything we have done has been well deserved, I'm sure!" He relaxed a bit and forced a smile. "But please, let us not talk of war. I would much rather hear your voice speak of sweeter things."

I blushed. "Very well, you know best." I breathed easier with the reassurance that the British were not as cruel as I had feared.

Before I could resume my reading, however, Mr. Kingsley knocked and entered.

Lawrence had his back to the door and had to turn around to see who it was. "You do have a habit of interrupting, Mr. Kingsley," he said rather curtly and faced me again.

Eric's jaw tightened. "My apologies, Lieutenant. I was not aware you were calling upon Miss Devonshire." He turned to go.

"Wait," I called, letting the book fall to my lap. "What is it you wanted?"

He looked at me, then at Lawrence, and back at me. "I was wondering if you knew where I might find a book on winter birds on the island. I have looked all over the library but have had no luck."

I looked at him curiously and he winked back. I was thankful Lawrence could not see it and that Mary Ann was still busy with her playing. I had to be careful not to let my own face reveal too much of the message Eric was sending to me. He wanted me to meet him in the library later.

"I am sure we have one. Perhaps it is by the large window?" I replied, showing I had understood his meaning and would come to the seats in the nook when I could.

"Thank you." He nodded and left the room.

"Really, does he have nothing better to do than to read books like that?" Lawrence scoffed.

༺༻

As soon as Lawrence had left, I hurried to the library and found Eric waiting patiently in one of the two chairs reading a book.

"Sorry to have kept you waiting." He stood abruptly.

"What are you reading?"

"A book about winter birds on Long Island." He grinned and we sat. "What is it you wanted to see me about?"

"I wanted to let you know that the Miltons will be leaving early tomorrow morning on a whaling boat for Fairfield."

"Oh! That's wonderful!" I was glad to hear their dangerous journey would be over soon, and that we would no longer have to worry for our own sakes that they were at Penningcoll. "Are they in need of any food or supplies?"

"No, I have already had a friend help with that."

"Really? Who?" I could no more easily think of anyone I knew who would be willing to help Patriot refugees now than before.

"Let us just say he believes it his Christian duty to support the innocent people who have been punished unjustly."

I respected his desire for secrecy and instead asked another question. "Then answer me this: how ever did you find out that the Miltons were hiding at Penningcoll? And how did the house seem so prepared for their coming? I mean, when I first came, there was firewood and food and water."

He looked out the window, and I could see him struggle for a moment. "Do you really want to know? Once I tell you I cannot take it back."

I hesitated, but I still nodded my head.

"Very well." He took a deep breath and looked back at the door before continuing. "I have contact with… an informant who told me they were in need of refuge and transportation. When they arrived, I found out that they had had a little trouble along the way, which was why Mr.

IN THE WAITING

Milton's leg was injured. Thankfully they managed to hide in a barn before making it the rest of the way to Penningcoll. I am sorry I had to drag you into this, but I didn't know what else to do, and I was afraid if I told you who they were beforehand you wouldn't have come with me."

"No, don't apologize. You are probably right, but once I saw them, I couldn't refuse." A silence passed between us before we both began speaking at the same time. Once again silence fell. "Please," I said, "continue."

"Well, the Miltons are not the only ones who need help. Penningcoll was set up to be a safe haven for patriot refugees and for couriers bringing spy messages to General Washington. I have agreed to facilitate these matters with the guidance of my informant."

"Who set up Penningcoll? And how do you have access to it?" I interrupted. Now that my curiosity had begun to be fed, I didn't want to stop digging for details.

"That, I'm afraid, is a story for another time. For now, I would like to ask if you would be willing to continue, not only protecting the secret of Penningcoll, but also helping those who stay at Penningcoll. Of course, I understand if you do not wish to put your reputation and, dare I say, safety on the line, so if you must refuse…"

"You have helped me begin to see the truth of this terrible war. I would gladly continue to do what I can to help the innocent."

"Thank you." He looked deep into my eyes, and I could feel how much he meant it. "You know," he went on, shifting in his seat, as if to signify a change in subject, "I am happy to hear you are finally thinking about this for yourself. But which side of the war you support is not the only decision that needs to be made on one's own. Marriage is also such a decision."

I didn't answer. The moment during which I had actually felt a connection to this man was quickly gone. What business of his was it whom I marry?

We sat for a moment before he continued softly. "I do understand a little of what you are going through with the pressures from your family, you know. They want you to think a certain way and to succeed at the goals they set for you. It can be hard to take a step back and see what you are actually meant to do."

I looked at him and saw his shoulders droop under what I saw as the weight of memory. "You and Lieutenant Taylor seem to be getting rather close," he commented and cleared his throat.

"Yes." I blushed as I thought of the time the Lieutenant and I had recently spent together. "I'm glad we have. As I have confided in you, I do need to marry well for my family's sake, and it seems the Lieutenant might be my chance to do that."

"But how do you feel about him? I mean, as I said, marriage is not a decision that should be made for you."

I shifted uncomfortably in my seat. I had grown more accustomed to Eric's forward questions, but this was too personal, even coming from him. I should not have let the subject continue and should not have begun to reveal my feelings to him.

"Is it really so hard to believe that a successful officer would find me attractive and desire a future with me?" I demanded, then looked away in what I believed to be righteous anger.

"Charlotte…" He waited for me to face him. When I did, I was expecting to see an expression of mischief and curiosity, but instead his gray eyes were filled with concern and care. "I don't want to see you get hurt."

I was caught off guard by this. It did not fit the picture

IN THE WAITING

I had of his character. Why should he care so much about what happened to me? "Thank you," I finally replied. "I appreciate your concern, but I have every reason to believe the Lieutenant is genuine in his feelings for me and every reason to receive, encourage, and enjoy his attention."

Eric nodded once, then looked out the window with narrowed eyes and bit his tongue.

Chapter 13

When the time came for Bridgett and her small family to leave, I was there at Penningcoll to wish them goodbye.

"Have a safe journey," I said. "And when this war is over, and it is possible once more, come back and visit Longford so I might have you as a true guest."

"Oh, I'd like that very much, Miss Charlotte. Thank you again for your help. God will bless you for your kind work and will guide us all toward a future of freedom."

"I hope so." I smiled. I still wasn't used to the idea of agreeing with Patriots. "We had better be going," Eric said, coming towards us.

Bridgett moved to situate herself under the covering in the back of the wagon with her father and son.

"Make sure they get on board all right," I told him quietly. "And make sure you stay out of trouble," I added with a nervous smile.

He lifted his arm as if about to embrace me, but he dropped it again and answered, "Don't worry, I will." He hopped up on the seat and drove away.

∞

Time passed quickly for many weeks. Lawrence called as often as he could, though his duties as Lieutenant kept him busy. Eric and I helped another Patriot use Penningcoll as a safe haven on his journey. He was a courier bringing a

IN THE WAITING

message from New York to Connecticut.

He came in the middle of the night, and if Eric had not come knocking at my bedroom door to tell me, I would never have known he had come. He came and went so quickly.

"I thought you might like to meet him," Eric whispered to me through the narrow opening in my door. "He is a genuine spy, and I know your curious nature."

I raised an eyebrow, but conceded, "I would, yes. I will be right out."

When I had dressed and the two of us had snuck out of the house, we hurried to Penningcoll but did not use horses, as that would have aroused the stablehand.

The young spy was waiting for us and let us in immediately.

"I hear you have been of great help to our cause, Miss Devonshire," he said. "I thank you." He bowed.

I blushed. "It is an honor to serve, and it is an honor to meet you, sir." I met British officers all the time, but to meet a man instrumental to the other side was new and exciting.

"Oh, I'm no 'sir,' ma'am. Sam'ill do just fine." He blushed a little.

"Sam," Mr. Kingsley began, "what news do you bring to General Washington?"

"I don't rightly know, sir. I was given a sealed letter and instructions not to open it, but to get it to the Fairfield as soon as possible, where the next courier will take it by land the rest of the way to the General."

"You mean you are risking your life to carry a letter without even knowing its contents?" I asked in wonder.

"I may not know what is in the letter, or what good it will do. It might not be of any use by the time it reaches Washington. But I do know that freedom is worth whatever risk is asked of me. Like that Patrick Henry said, 'Give me liberty, or give me death.'"

I marveled that there did not seem to be an ounce of fear in this young man's voice, only determination and conviction. It must be nice, I thought, to be so sure of something that it mattered not what price it cost. Though I was willing to help the Patriots, and almost willing to call myself one, I was not so confident as to risk so much. I imagined the worst that could happen if anyone caught me doing what I was doing would be that I would have to lie to salvage my reputation. In my mind, that would be bad enough.

"I pray, then, that your courage will be rewarded." Eric assured him, "If all goes well, you will be on the boat and on your way to the safety of Connecticut by dawn."

All did go as planned, so Eric was back at Longford before breakfast. No one had missed either of us during the night.

Our work at Penningcoll was not the only task to attend. I faced Mother's weekly reminder to snare Lawrence and Father's frequent disappearances for the sake of his business.

Spring came, and with it bloomed the apple blossoms. The orchard once again became a common place of refuge for when I felt most in need of escaping either the pressures that came with the secrets I bore or those that came from having spent months accepting Lawrence's advances only to be waiting still for a proposal.

As happened every year when the weather warmed, we received several visitors to Longford who had been invigorated by the sunshine. Among these visitors were the Barlow ladies.

IN THE WAITING

"And how are you and Lieutenant Taylor getting along?" Mrs. Barlow asked between sips of tea. Mother looked at me expectantly.

"He and I have been getting to know one another," I replied, unsure of how else I could appropriately reply to the older woman's question.

"But you are not yet engaged?" Sarah pressed.

"That is strange," chimed Ellen. "He seemed to be quite eager for a wife when I was with him in New York last autumn."

"What do you mean, Ellen? Why would you know such things?" I asked, with probably more intensity than I intended.

"Well, he escorted me to most of the dinners and balls, and he was attentive in all the ways a man would be who desired a woman—as a wife, of course." She blushed.

I became flustered but couldn't think of how to respond, so I returned to drinking my tea and kept my thoughts to myself. Thankfully Mary Ann changed the subject.

"Tell me again about the dances you went to in New York, Ellen. I think I will simply die if Father does not let me go this year." The conversation continued and covered all the usuals of social events past and future, but I heard little of it. My thoughts dwelt too much on the man whom I hoped to marry and still somehow, at times, felt I barely knew. I was able to convince myself that there could be no other reason for him giving Ellen such attention but that he wished to pay her a kindness out of the goodness of his heart. He was tender in that way, and I would not expect him to let a young lady be without an escort.

On another day that my father was not at home, Miss

Ada Winters came to visit. Mother was out visiting a neighbor with Mary Ann, and so I was left to receive her alone.

"Hello, Ada." I gestured to a seat, bewildered at her presence. "How are you on this fine day?" Why would she want to visit me? I knew what she thought of me. She had made it quite clear last Christmas Eve.

"Fine."

I waited for her to continue, but it took several minutes. We just sat in awkward silence, listening to the birds outside.

"I was under the impression Mr. Kingsley was still staying with your family." "He is, but he is not at home right now."

"Oh."

"Is there a message I can take for him?" My curiosity regarding her intentions was certainly piqued.

"No, I just thought I might give myself the pleasure of spending the afternoon with him.

But if he is not around, I suppose I can come back."

So that was it. Ada was bored with her other men and thought she could entangle herself with Eric. Anger rose within me. My reaction must have come from a feeling of responsibility to protect my family from the potential disaster that Ada posed for our reputation, for it really was none of my business what Mr. Kingsley did in his spare time.

I took a deep breath and tried to speak coolly. "I thought you didn't like him. At least that was what he told me."

She was quiet and her eyes narrowed.

"Regardless, you would be wasting your time coming back here, and I will kindly ask you not to, so long as your intentions remain the same."

IN THE WAITING

"You're just jealous! You're afraid I might actually turn his head when you haven't been able to do so after living in the same house as him for months!"

"How do you know?" I spat. I stood quickly and spun on my heel. She clumsily rose and followed me to the foyer. I opened the front door. "Good day, Miss Winters."

Her mouth was wide open, but she left without saying another word.

I hastened through the house to the back door. I needed a walk in the orchard. How dare she suggest that I desire that kind of relationship with Mr. Kingsley? Perhaps I should not have implied what I had, but I was so tired of Ada's haughty attitude. And besides, if he wasn't so incorrigible and I actually wanted to, I'm sure I could turn his head. Yes, my father had seemed to desire a closeness to develop between us, but I am sure his only hope now would be for us to be good friends because of our fathers' friendship. There is no way anyone could seriously believe that we could think of each other in any more intimate way at this point.

I lifted my face to the sun and let its warmth and the sounds of spring calm me. I remembered what Eric had said about not letting what Ada said bother me so much. The good opinions of people like her were not worth fretting over. It made me feel better. I smiled as I recalled my first opinion of Mr. Kingsley. It was not exactly that he had proved me wrong about his character, but I could admit to myself at least that he had several times been the source of sound advice. He had not only helped me see the value in the colonists' fight for freedom, but had also given me the opportunity to use my interest in medicine, and my spare time, for a good cause. I appreciated this more than I had ever expected.

"Charlotte?"

I turned, expecting to see Eric, and jumped when instead Lawrence stood in front of me. "Oh!"

"I'm sorry to startle you. When I didn't find you in the house, that Mr. Kingsley said I might find you here."

That Mr. Kingsley indeed. So, he was back at Longford. It was lucky I did not know he was to be back today, or I might not have been able to be rid of Miss Winters so easily. Why would he send Lawrence out here when he knew I would be unchaperoned? He had always seemed so uneasy and untrusting of Lieutenant Taylor.

"I see."

"I believe he watched me every step of the way from the widow's walk where I first looked for you and instead found him."

I smiled to myself. No, Eric had not lost his concern. I had no doubt he was still standing there waiting for us to emerge again. I had no reason not to trust Lawrence, but for Mr.

Kingsley's sake I suggested that we take our walk back out of the orchard and towards the bay. "Whatever you wish, Charlotte." Lawrence offered his arm.

Sure enough, when we emerged, I could make out Eric's form at the top of the house. I thought I even saw him tip his hat before he disappeared from the edge.

I decided that now was as good a time as any to ask about what I had learned of Lawrence a few days previous. "Lawrence, the ladies of the Barlow family were here the other day."

"How nice," he commented good-naturedly.

"Ellen said you spent quite a bit of time with her when you were in New York last fall.

That was nice of you."

"Thank you, but I cannot take credit for it. Sir Barlow asked me to look after his sister." "I see. Well, from what she says, it seems you enjoyed your task."

He looked down at me. "Yes," he answered slowly, trying to discover any hidden motives in my questioning. "Ellen is a lovely girl and plenty of fun, but trust me when I say you are worlds better." He stopped and turned me to face him. "*Your* support and affection are what I desire most." He stepped closer and I shivered from the sea breeze coming up the cliff edge where we now stood.

His answer satisfied me for the moment, but I felt I needed to press him on the implications of what he was saying. Mother would not be content with only hints. "I appreciate what you tell me, and I am flattered by your attention, but may I ask what your plans are for the future?"

"I'm sorry, Charlotte, but I cannot say anything definite until the war is over. I don't know how my position will be changing. I hope you can understand."

"Of course, Lawrence. I can be patient." I gave him a half smile and chided myself for doubting his faithfulness and love.

"Thank you, darling." He pulled me even closer till his lips were nearly to mine.

"Isn't it a lovely spring day?" I leaned away uncomfortably. I had never been kissed, and I had always thought I would save it for my engagement. He slowly released his arms from about my waist.

"Yes, it is." But his eyes didn't move from my face.

Chapter 14

No sooner had Eric returned than did he leave once more. I couldn't imagine where my father was sending him all the time, but I was glad that there was never a need to use Penningcoll while he was away.

"I do hope you are not taking advantage of Mr. Kingsley," I told Father as we traveled to church one Sunday, "nor working too hard yourself. It seems you are both gone quite often."

"I appreciate your concern, dear, but trust me, I have things under control." He squeezed my hand and smiled. "I will, however, take his place more often if you tell me you are beginning to prefer his company to mine." He raised his eyebrows.

"Father! Of course not!"

"Well I would not be disappointed to find you did." His eyes searched mine, but Mother replied before I could.

"She certainly *should* prefer another man's company to yours at this point in her life, but that man is *not* Mr. Kingsley. It is Lieutenant Taylor." She smiled rather triumphantly.

Mary Ann squeezed my knee in excitement, and Father's expression changed to take on a more serious air.

"Is that so?"

"I must concede that I am very fond of the Lieutenant's company, but I could never admit to you that I preferred

IN THE WAITING

his to yours." I tried to ease the growing tension I felt by laughing lightly.

He smiled softly as we halted in front of the church and stepped from the carriage.

We took our seats as the organist began to play. That morning's sermon was about the wrath of God and the promise of judgment upon those who turn their backs to Him. The minister paid close attention to addressing the fact that the rebel patriots who were showing such greed and rage, as well as all who helped them, would be among the first to feel God's hatred.

I felt a little sick to my stomach as we stepped outside at the close of service. It was difficult to enjoy the fine spring day and catch up with our friends after hearing such condemnation of actions that I had convinced myself stemmed from a godly compassion. My stomach only lurched harder when I scanned the lawn and saw Ada viewing me with ridicule. She looked quickly away when she saw I had caught her, and I felt a little proud of myself for leaving such an impression last we spoke. I did hope, though, that Ada would not try to mar my reputation, like she had on Christmas Eve, out of spite for my keeping her from making a fool of Mr. Kingsley.

Before I could dwell too much on the situation I might have created for myself, Mrs.

Barlow came up with Lady Sarah to say hello.

"Good day, Mr. Devonshire, Mrs. Devonshire, Miss Devonshire. Miss Mary Ann," she addressed, noticing my sister had been scanning the yard, "Ellen is under the tree over there, and I am sure she is eager to see you." She smiled warmly.

"Thank you, ma'am," she replied and hurried away to find her friend.

"Hello, Mrs. Barlow," replied Mother. She extended

her hands, and Mrs. Barlow took them in greeting.

"And where is Mr. Kingsley this morning?"

"He is off on business for a few days," Father answered.

"Oh, it seems you have been keeping him quite busy, Mr. Devonshire. I must say I am rather surprised he has stayed at Longford so long. I would have thought if he planned to help you for so long, he would find his own accommodations."

"Yes," chimed in Sarah Barlow, "it must be rather tiresome to have a guest such as him for so long, especially when he is not a relative."

"His father was like a brother to me, and young Mr. Kingsley has been a great help. I am glad he has been able to stay as long as he has," replied my father. "He is not merely an employee."

"Ah, I see. Then he has been getting along well?" She glanced sideways at me. "Certainly. He has been a joy to have around. Hasn't he, Charlotte?"

I just nodded dumbly, hoping Sarah's question had not stemmed from a conversation with Miss Winters.

Mrs. Barlow looked at my mother, who was choosing to keep her opinions on the matter to herself, and Lady Barlow just turned up her nose.

"What an excellent sermon today," interjected Mother, apparently tired of Mr. Kingsley being the topic of conversation.

"Oh yes," Sarah agreed heartily. "What a joy it is to be reminded so often that we are standing on God's side of this war." She sighed rather pathetically.

"Hmm, yes indeed," her mother-in-law added.

"God's wrath is most assuredly nothing to take lightly," said Father. "One certainly must take care never to incite it and always to strive to do what is right in His eyes, regardless of the cost."

IN THE WAITING

"Yes, and to think these colonists are willing to risk judgment just to avoid paying the cost of a few taxes." Mother shook her head.

I had never been so uncomfortable with the subject as I was then, and I was happy when the conversation once again shifted.

"Oh, and I have not seen Lieutenant Taylor yet. Is he here today, Charlotte?" Mrs.

Barlow's eyes began searching the crowd.

"I do not believe so, ma'am. He has told me he often has duties that last far into the night on Saturday evenings, and he is not always able to make it to service as a result."

"That is perfectly understandable. After all, his service to his country is a service to God, according to what the minister said." Her words were reassuring, but I still wished Lawrence had come today. It seemed more often than not he missed church, and I was disappointed by the fact that I could not be seen with him more often in public. Perhaps it was selfish of me, but I couldn't help it. He was a well sought after man, and I believed I was succeeding in 'securing a future with him,' as my mother would say.

❦

The next afternoon was bright and warm, so I decided to go for a ride around both our land and the Penningcoll property. I reached the top of a rise on the road to town, and I could overlook the valley between the two houses. I breathed deeply of the fresh spring air and closed my eyes. I leaned forward and whispered in Marble's ear, "How would you like to run?"

I went faster than was fitting for a lady, but as I was alone, I didn't much care. There was a small wood on the other side of Penningcoll, and I had an inkling to go there and daydream for a while. When I reached the wood,

I found a large maple tree with a soft bed of new grass beneath. I tethered Marble to a branch and laid down with my hands behind my head.

I thought of my wedding day. Picturing the proud faces of my father and mother brought a smile to my face. I felt myself walking down the aisle, but when I turned my eyes to the altar, there was no one there. I sighed. The one flaw in my dream was that that was all it was: a dream. I turned my thoughts instead to Lieutenant Taylor. I saw him in his bright red uniform, holding my hand as I lighted the sleigh. This was better. If only he would propose. It was not that I doubted him. He was a gentleman and would not be leading me to believe marriage was his intention if it was not. I did, however, doubt myself. I was sure he would at some point see that I was not worth my lack of a dowry or that I would say or do something to mess it all up.

My thoughts drifted back to the sleighride I had shared with Lawrence. I pictured him lean towards me as he had, only this time I did not turn away. I let myself succumb to him and melted as his lips touched mine.

I held my eyes tightly closed, and a breeze wisped through the grass and blew across my face. I heard a twig crack and sitting up quickly, gasped.

A man stepped out from behind a tree. "Sorry!" he said. It was Eric! "I didn't mean to frighten you." He walked towards me and smiled almost laughingly. I became acutely aware of how indecent I looked. I raised a hand to my hair and felt several blades of grass woven through it.

"Oh, I must look quite a mess! What are you doing here?" I was perhaps unduly annoyed with him.

"I was about to ask you the same thing." He grinned mischievously and sat down beside me before I had a

IN THE WAITING

chance to stand.

"Well I, I was just relaxing, that's all." My cheeks were flushed with frustration, and I looked away.

"Ah." He leaned back on his elbow and started picking at the grass.

I adjusted myself to sit more appropriately and covered my protruding shoes with my skirts.

"I thought," he continued, "that you were laying here dreaming of your Lawrence." He ripped a blade in two while his gaze similarly pierced me.

I blushed and made a clumsy effort to stand. It was not as dramatic as I had intended because he stood as well to help me gain my footing on the soft ground.

"Have you been to the house yet?"

"No," he answered, leaving his previous comment alone. "I have just come across the sound and thought I would take a walk before seeing everyone."

I stepped around him to get to Marble.

"Well, I am glad you are back safe and sound." Though I did not invite it, he lifted me onto the saddle. "Unsettling news of the war comes all too often. I know how dangerous it is for you even to be here."

"So, you're saying you missed me?" He looked at me sideways as he placed my foot in the stirrup.

I pretended not to hear. I was reluctant to admit it to myself and was not about to say so in front of my family when Father had asked that Sunday morning, for they would have misunderstood. But I was growing rather fond of Eric's company and, when he was gone, did occasionally miss the intrigue he brought to my life. His lack of pomp and ceremony was surprisingly refreshing. I was used to giving so much attention to how I appeared to others, but with Eric, I had no pressure to impress him, and I was sure that I could do nothing that would improve, or worsen for that matter, the relatively negative view he probably still had of me. I also appreciated that he did not shy away from the deeper topics. I realized with some regret that I could not recall a single time I had discussed anything of any real, weighty significance with Lawrence.

"Charlotte?" The sound of my name drew me back to reality. "Yes? Sorry."

"I just wanted to let you know that I have received word that another messenger will be coming to Penningcoll in a few days. The route he was supposed to take has been compromised."

"We will need to replenish the supplies and clean up a bit before he arrives," I said matter-of-factly.

He appeared pleased I had volunteered without him having to ask. "Tomorrow morning after breakfast?"

"I will meet you in the orchard then."

"Thank you, Charlotte. I appreciate your help. I shall see you at dinner tonight." I nodded in acknowledgement and clicked my tongue to Marble.

Chapter 15

Lieutenant Taylor joined us for dinner that evening. I was glad to see him. "And how are things for you, Lieutenant?" Father asked.

"Ah, quite well!" He wiped his mouth with his napkin. "Just the other day I apprehended a farmer who was harboring Patriot spies just on the other side of Setauket."

"Oh dear!" exclaimed Mother, "How terrifying to think such things are happening so close to our homes. I am glad you caught him."

"And what is to be done with him?" my father inquired.

"He is to be hanged for treason." A silence fell over the room. Eric gave me a look that reminded me of what he had said earlier about the route that had been compromised.

"It is a shame for his wife and daughter," Lawrence continued, "but he should have thought of that before dealing in criminal matters."

"What will they do?" I asked with concern.

"Oh, I am sure they will be fine. They seem not to have been aware of what had been going on, so we are letting them go. And besides, his daughter is rather beautiful and should be able to marry well enough, if she can recover from the shame her father brought upon her."

I shifted uncomfortably and caught Eric's gaze. His eyes were filled with knowing and sorrowful compassion.

I knew he understood that I would feel this girl's pain in a unique way.

The conversation moved to other matters, but my thoughts could not move on so quickly.

While I was certainly upset at these sad tidings, I did not blame Lawrence for them. He was doing his duty and what he believed to be right. It was a mark of good character. But then, of course, there was the matter that this man sitting across from me, who seemed to be concerned for my reaction to this news, was in impeccable danger himself. I thanked God that Eric had come home safely, and prayed He would continue to protect us as we sought to give shelter to those who were in need of it. Despite what the minister had said, I wanted, perhaps needed, to believe we were doing what God desired us to.

∞

We took extra care to make sure we were not seen as we went to Penningcoll the next morning. When I met Mr. Kingsley at our designated spot, he was ready with a small cart of supplies hitched to his horse, and I was mounted on Marble. I had brought a couple medical books along too, thinking I might have time to stop in the woods on the way home for a quiet read. We paused often to listen for anyone who might be following us and often looked to check the ridges from which we might be spotted. I was particularly grateful at that moment that the open field beyond the orchard was not visible from any main road.

Once we arrived, we began unloading the supplies.

"Where did all this come from anyway?" I asked as he worked to get the door open with his hands much too full of loose items.

"A generous friend." He managed to open the door, but several things dropped to the ground. "A generous friend who would rather not be named," he added before I had a chance to inquire further. He knew I would be curious like the last time he had given me a similar answer.

"Very well. I suppose I can live with it," I replied slyly when he came back to the cart. I dug through the bandages, blankets, and cans of food. "It is very good that we have all these things. You never know what we will need."

He took a deep breath and smiled. "And you never know when we will need your medical expertise again either." He was opening my satchel and had found the books.

I blushed and hurried to snatch the books back out of his hands. "I would appreciate more opportunities to put some of my knowledge to use. I know I can't expect to use it anywhere in the real world."

He paused before lifting another crate from the cart. "Is this not the real world?"

"Well, no, of course not. If it were the real world, I wouldn't be unchaperoned with you here, let alone helping with such a scandalous endeavor, and the people we help here would be as hopeless as they should be. After all, there is no way the Patriots will win, and, quite frankly, I'm shocked neither of us have yet been caught. You know how dangerous this is."

I did not mean to sound so serious, but it really was serious, and a weight hung in the air between us.

"So, you are saying you have justified going against your parents and the whole of society by helping Patriots, and doing so in this capacity with me, because you considered it part of a fantasy world?"

I couldn't tell whether Mr. Kingsley was more bewildered or appalled, but I chose to believe the former. I carried a bundle inside, Eric following close behind. "Well, yes," I answered, "I have conceded to appreciating the plight of the colonists, but you can't expect me to admit such complete rebellion to who I am."

"Who you are, or who your mother says you are?"

I spun around to face him, but I had to turn away, for I had never seen such a piercing look in his eyes before. I was afraid he would see right through me, or worse, open the door for me to see myself. I had worked hard to rationalize my actions and could not deal with the repercussions of admitting myself to be a true Patriot.

"I may no longer be able to call myself a committed Loyalist," I said more demurely, "but I cannot call myself a Patriot."

He lifted a crate and headed back inside. "At least not out loud," I added.

He paused in the doorway before continuing. He had heard me, but I was glad he did not continue to press.

I took a deep breath, considering the difficult subject closed for the time being, and followed Eric inside.

"I have enjoyed having the Lieutenant around so often." I knew it was not the best of topics for Mr. Kingsley, but at least it was a change. "He really is such a gentleman. Don't you think so?" I asked as I took up the broom, knowing the answer was likely 'no.' "I mean, it is such an honor to receive an officer such as himself into our home. It is not as if I, I mean we, have deserved such attention."

"Mhmm," Mr. Kingsley replied casually as he began wetting a rag.

I was annoyed at this response. It still bothered me how much Eric seemed to dislike Lawrence. Something told me there was more to it than their difference in loyalties. "Did you hear that the Lieutenant is being awarded a great honor for his service? He was so nonchalant when he told me. He really is such a humble man." I turned to Eric, searching for some sort of approval.

IN THE WAITING

He noticed my silence and looked up to give me a weak, almost pained smile, before returning to wiping down the table.

"Did he also hang the moon?" he mumbled under his breath.

I shot him a disapproving look. "No matter your differences in beliefs, you ought to speak about a gentleman such as Lawrence with more respect."

"Well, I will say he reminds me of my father," he said.

I was happy to hear Eric compliment Lawrence. "I'm sure that's high praise."

He offered me a rather pitying look with raised eyebrows before he continued. "I certainly see you have had no trouble looking past such differences in belief, though I know them to be greater than you will admit. I wonder if he would do the same," Eric replied.

"And what is that supposed to mean?"

"I am simply pointing out that perhaps the Lieutenant might not be quite as smitten if he knew…" he let the thought hang unfinished.

"Our love is not as fragile as that." I walked confidently from the house to bring in more supplies, and he followed.

"Here, let me help you." Mr. Kingsley took the last crate, which was particularly heavy, from me as I tried to lift it from the cart.

"Thank you," I replied without making eye contact. His nearness made me feel small and ridiculous in my arguments. I instead took in some of the firewood that had been stacked outside.

I was lowering my load onto the hearth when the back of my hand scraped the edge of the sharp bricks. "Ouch!" I exclaimed, as I clumsily dropped the logs and grasped the bleeding wound.

Mr. Kingsley hurried towards me and gently took

my hand in his. I had never noticed how large his hands were compared to mine. He held my hand face up in his as if he was holding a delicate flower and inspected my palm. He led me to the wash basin and gingerly rinsed my cuts. Though it stung considerably, I remained silent. He reached for one of the bandages sitting on the table and drew nearer as he began wrapping the hand.

We were then standing so close that I could feel the warmth of his breath through my wispy hair. There was still tension between us, but this was somehow different. I raised my head and studied his face. He seemed to be deep in thought, as if contemplating again a question he had asked himself often. I lowered my gaze back to my hand. He glanced up at me once he finished. He stood silent for a moment, still holding my hand, as if waiting for me to pull it away, yet hoping I wouldn't. "Miss Devonshire, you said once that you liked to dance when there were gentlemen with whom to do it."

I nodded, curious as to where this was going.

"And though we have danced once since you made that remark, I knew you did not enjoy it, and perhaps you, well, even hated me for it. I know you have never considered me a gentleman."

I remained silent, unsure of what point he was about to make. I had learned to be on my guard with Mr. Kingsley.

"Would you consider me one now?"

I was not prepared for this. "Well, I...." I froze, not even knowing myself what my answer was.

I thought about taking a step back, but he grasped my hand more tightly and reached his other out, placing it in the small of my back which kept me from fleeing. My heart began to race. He took a shaky breath and whispered, "Miss Devonshire... Charlotte, would you... may I... have this dance?"

IN THE WAITING

I breathed in sharply. I was stunned. This was not the Mr. Kingsley I knew, who was honorable but rough. This was a tender and chivalrous gentleman. I was simply in awe. I nodded dumbly, allowing him to draw me to the center of the room.

"But we have no music." I started to feel rather silly.

"Do you not hear the birds? Can you not feel the beating of my heart? It is like listening to the prettiest music in the world when I look at you."

I was so surprised I was at a loss for words. This man, whom I had believed thought rather lowly of me and whom I had thought to be uncouth and brash, was revealing himself to be a romantic who rivaled even Lieutenant Taylor.

He stepped lightly, spinning me around gracefully. Time seemed to stand still. That dance was one of the best I had ever enjoyed. It felt like gliding through clouds. I did not have to think about the steps or what I was doing. I couldn't have even if I had wanted to. As I looked into his eyes and he spun me around that old room, everything else seemed to disappear. He pulled me closer, and I closed my eyes.

When I opened them, suddenly, the realization that this *was* the real world came into focus. I gasped and pushed Eric away, rushing to the other side of the room with my back to him.

"What's wrong?" he asked, stepping towards me with an outstretched hand.

"Oh, what would my mother say?" I spoke more to myself than to him. "What would Father say?" Then I really started to panic. "What would Lawerence say?"

Eric stopped where he was and bowed his head.

"How could I have done this to him!" I breathed heavily in confusion and frustration. "I need to go," I said, turning to the door.

"Charlotte, wait!"

I stopped at the door but did not face him.

"Please forgive me. I should not have... I'm sorry." I felt heavy, but I raised my head and left for home.

༄

Eric was not at tea that afternoon, and I was quite relieved. I did not wish to face him and did not know what I should have said if I had. It was out of confusion and embarrassment that I did not wish to see him. It was not that I blamed him for what happened. Perhaps I should have, but I couldn't. I had enjoyed those few moments too much to blame anyone but myself. What was wrong with me? I loved Lawrence. Was our love really so fragile as to be shaken by one encounter with another man? I looked out my window and saw Mr. Kingsley finally returning to the yard. I made a promise to myself to forget what had happened and start taking more care to give my attention to Lawrence, with whom rested my hope of a successful marriage and the security of my family. I went to bed that night with more questions than answers and slept fitfully.

Chapter 16

I woke up with no more clarity of thought. After the incident with Eric, it was only right that I doubted my own love for Lawrence. I felt overwhelming guilt for what had happened.

More accurately, I felt overwhelming guilt for enjoying what had happened as much as I did. I went over it several times in my head. Did I unintentionally give him some sign of encouragement? Did he actually care for me, or was he just using me? Maybe his explanation for what had happened with Ada was indeed a lie. No, I couldn't believe that. I was sure this was my fault. I should never have agreed to be with him in such improper circumstances, whether I considered it a part of my true reality or not. I vowed to be more cautious in the future. Mr. Kingsley was right about at least one thing: our work at Penningcoll and the time I had spent with him *was* real life, and I had to face what that meant.

On top of my own guilt, what Mr. Kingsley had said about Lawrence's attention still unnerved me. I did not doubt his love as much as I doubted his reason for loving me. I did not deserve it, especially after my recent actions. Why *would* he wish to marry me? The only possibility I saw was that he really did love me, but how could a man like him love a woman like me?

I knew I needed more time to think, but that would

have to come later. Lawrence was waiting for me in the garden. Mother had invited him to come for breakfast, and he had said he wished to speak with me beforehand. I did not want to be late.

ௐ

I found him sitting on one of the benches by the fountain, now bubbling merrily in the warm, spring sun.

"Charlotte!" he exclaimed, standing to his feet. "Thank you for coming. I know I see you rather often, but I still find myself longing for you when I am not with you."

I blushed and took his outstretched hand. He sat me down beside him.

"Oh, Lawrence, you always know just what to say. How did I ever earn your attention?" My voice was light, but my heart was in earnest.

"What a silly question," he chuckled.

"I mean it, Lawrence. Why is it you seem to care for me so deeply? After all, I am not particularly beautiful, and you know I am not wealthy."

"You're serious." His words were more an observation than a question. "Well," he began, sitting up straighter and looking toward the trees, "you are pretty, no matter what others say, and I suppose you just make me feel like a man ought. You give me confidence and pride, but you are not as delicate as some other women who need constant pampering."

I wasn't sure what to say, but it all seemed quite complimentary, so I smiled. "Well, you are a man on whose arm any woman should be proud to be."

He beamed and reached for my other hand, now holding both of mine in his on his knee. I can describe his presence at that moment in only one word: *intoxicating*. He moved closer and leaned towards me. I knew he was

IN THE WAITING

trying to kiss me. The thought made my heart race even faster than it had been. It was both exciting and a little scary to be sitting so near a man who had such thoughts on his mind. Despite my daydreams of not so long ago, I turned my head slightly to elude his advance. He slowly reached his hand up to my cheek, touching it softly and drawing my gaze back to his.

"What is it, Charlotte?" he whispered. "Don't be afraid."

I could feel his breath through my hair, and he put an arm around my waist. "Lawrence, no." I put my hand on his chest to push him away, but I couldn't find the strength. I sat watching my hand rise and fall with his breathing, confused at my own inability to do what I knew I ought. I cleared my throat. "Not until you have proposed." I tried to sound resolved, though I am sure I sounded rather pitiful.

Lawrence sighed heavily, but let me go, and we both stood. He combed a hand through his silky, black hair as he turned away. After a moment, he spun back around and, reaching for my hand, said matter-of-factly, "Then marry me."

"Lawrence," I replied in a whisper, "do you mean it?" I was shocked. I mean, of course I had been hoping and waiting for this moment for months, but I had nearly resigned myself to thinking it would never come.

He took a deep breath. "Yes," he assured me, in all sincerity. "Please marry me. You have been a joy to me these last many months, and I do not know what I would do without you."

"You don't mind that I have no inheritance? No dowry?" I asked in hesitating hope.

"I will have a fortune of my own when the war ends and the rewards are given. I am sure enough of that now to make you an offer." He took my hands and placed them on his chest before putting his own around me. "I will need a woman by my side, and who better than you, you who have given me the tenderness I have needed." His lips brushed my neck. "Let me assure you that I see my sole purpose is to love you."

My heart fluttered and I submitted readily to his passionate kiss. His lips tasted like fine wine, and I drank deeply of them. He lifted me and laughed as he spun me through the air. A surge of happiness pulsed through me. I felt whole and complete. I had achieved what I desired most, a husband of worth who loved me. My dream was no longer just a dream. It was becoming real.

Still, something made me just a little uneasy about it. I felt guilty for keeping my thoughts about the war a secret from the man whom I cared for and who had just asked me to marry him, but I could not risk revealing the truth. I had a responsibility to my family to marry well, and I knew my mother would never forgive me if she knew I had ruined my chances with Lawrence. And that would be on top of all the other problems that would arise if my secret were to be made public. I had never been very good at squelching qualms enough to be able to do something I felt guilty about, so I decided the best course of action would be to stall until I could succeed in convincing myself to feel no guilt in saying yes.

"Lawrence..." I tried to catch my breath as he loosened his hold on me. "Would it be alright with you if I gave you my final answer tomorrow?"

He furrowed his eyebrows in concern and confusion, but conceded. "Certainly, my dear, whatever you need."

"Thank you," I said, looking deeply into those eyes to assure him of my sincerity and appreciation.

IN THE WAITING

Unfortunately, I was kept busy all morning with the family and our guest in the drawing room. Busy, that is, being present. It was not as if we did anything, or even talked of anything of significance, but it would have been rude of me to excuse myself when all knew it was for my sake that Lawrence was there. I did enjoy his company, of course, but I felt as if it was tainted by my uncertainty. I just wanted to sort out my life so that I could go back to enjoying it.

I had much to think about, and thankfully, following the noon meal, Mother was taking Mary Ann to Fencomb for a visit, so I would have some time to myself. I had declined accompanying them, excusing myself for the headache I did, in truth, have.

It was not until late that evening that I finally had a chance to sit down to do some serious contemplation about who I was and who I was going to be. First, was I a Patriot? My father had always taught Mary Ann and me to be compassionate and generous to those less fortunate than ourselves, so I did feel sorry for those suffering at the hands of the king, who had taxed them beyond what they are able to pay. I would be glad to see the British army take a step back from the innocent victims of the war. But these realizations did not lead me to believe I was a Patriot. To be that would require an agreement that King George III should let the colonies be free, or at least give them representation. Demanding representation did not make much sense to me. After all, we cannot demand power from God, so why should we demand it from our government? Of course, the king isn't God, but he is in authority, and humility would dictate submission.

I sat quietly, weighing my thoughts and feelings and their repercussions, for some time before coming to the conclusion that, for now at least, I could call myself a Patriot sympathizer, but not a Patriot. I could not see myself as a revolutionary, and certainly could not see myself standing in a place of such opposition to my family and friends.

Now that I had sorted that out, I needed to consider Lawrence's proposal. I was not in full agreement with him about the war, but I was not his enemy. He seemed to love me genuinely, and I believed I loved him too. I knew this was the chance I had been waiting for and working toward my whole life and that, if my mother knew, she would be furious I had not already accepted. Yet something held me back.

If I were to reject Lawrence, I would be not only alone once again, but also that much older, and with no suitors or prospects in sight. I might as well be resigning myself to spinsterhood — in other words, to failure. If I accepted him, my future as well as the future of my mother and sister would be set. I would have the positive opinion of all the fine ladies and gentlemen in the community and would soon have a home of my own of which I would be mistress. I would then be able to have and raise my own children, and most importantly, I would be loved. I would have a man always beside me who had committed himself to me. That was what I longed for. How could I possibly dismiss that chance?

There, I had convinced myself to say yes. At that moment, a sinking feeling in the pit of my stomach brought me back to uncertainty. It must just be nerves, I thought. I decided the decision could wait until morning when I had a clearer mind.

Chapter 17

I awoke the next morning, expecting joy to engulf me as it had the day before when I was in the arms of the man who loved me. I lay in bed, staring at the ceiling, waiting to feel that lightness and completeness that I had felt when he had pressed his lips to mine, but the feeling didn't come. Instead, I was left feeling rather empty. In fact, I could not have named a single emotion that I felt if someone had asked, though I knew I was full to the brim with them. I couldn't understand it. I had been offered the world I had dreamed of my whole life. Why was I finding it so hard to take it? I knew Lawrence would want an answer as soon as possible, so I got up and readied myself to take a walk along the beach to think until he arrived.

The sea air coming off the bay was salty and crisp. I closed my eyes and sought peace in the steady sound of the waves beating the shore.

"Charlotte?"

"Mr. Kingsley! I'm sorry, I didn't see you coming."

"It appears I have a knack for sneaking up on you." He came and stood beside me, facing the water. "What is it that has you lost in thought this time?" he asked.

I sighed and wrapped my shawl more closely around me against the cool wind. "I have a difficult decision to make."

"And what decision is that?" he pressed.

"Lieutenant Taylor has asked for my hand in marriage." I glanced at him, but his eyes remained fixed on the bay.

"I see, and why have you not yet given him an answer?" "Well, I mean, you and I…"

Then he looked at me. I searched his face to discover if it was hope or fear that I saw there, but I couldn't decide.

"You and I have done so much behind his back for the Patriot cause. How can I marry a man when I hold such a secret from him? Especially when he is a British officer."

He turned back to the water. "Do you want me to answer, or is this a rhetorical question?"

I was perplexed as to why Mr. Kingsley seemed to be so emotionless. I had reached the point of overflowing with emotion, and it was almost vexing to see him stand so unaffected by my situation. I hated to admit it, but I was rather disappointed he didn't appear to be jealous. I thought his previous tenderness had been at least a little genuine. Still, I told him I wanted his answer.

"If you are convinced of his love for you, and that he will honor you, and that you love him, then I suppose he will understand when someday you tell him of what you have been doing these past several months. And if you are sure of that, then what other reason is there for you to refuse him? You have made perfectly clear that your top priority in life is to secure your future in marriage."

"You are right. So, you think I should accept?"

His jaw stiffened. "I don't see why my opinion should matter so much to you."

I turned and stepped in front of him, so he could no longer avoid my gaze. "I would have hoped you would consider me a friend by now, Mr. Kingsley." I paused. "Why wouldn't I want your opinion?"

He swallowed hard and started to lean towards me.

IN THE WAITING

He stopped short and took a step back. "You've heard my answer," he said.

"Then I shall accept." I concluded with cautious cheerfulness, but I was a little confused.

If Eric was advising me to accept, I must have been wrong about Eric caring for me in any intimate way. I suppose I had completely misread what had transpired between us in Penningcoll. Perhaps Eric was really the rake I first thought him to be. As soon as I thought it, I knew it couldn't be true. I had seen too much of him to believe he was a man without honor. Still, it was very perplexing.

We walked side by side back towards the house.

"I should tell you that our expected guest has been delayed and may not arrive for some weeks," Eric said, "but I suppose you will want little to do with that now anyway, as you would not want to keep working behind the Lieutenant's back."

I nodded, sure that that would be the right decision. However, I was a little disappointed at the thought of stopping my work at Penningcoll.

༄

As soon as Lawrence came to the house that day, Mother, as usual, gave us the parlor to ourselves, and I was able to give him my answer.

"Have you thought anymore about what I asked?" he inquired. "Yes, I have."

"You should know that I have received your father's permission." Then he added a little more quietly, "Though I was surprised at the amount of convincing it took."

"I am glad, because I was going to say that as long as he approved, I would be happy to accept your offer."

His face lit up, and I smiled back.

"Oh, Charlotte!" He put his hands on my waist and lifted me effortlessly, spinning me around the room. "You don't know how much this means to me," he said, setting me down and caressing my cheek.

This was the feeling of joy I had been missing that morning. I drank it in and dreamed of the moments like these that would fill my life from now on.

"And don't worry about Father," I assured him as he drew me close. "He is just sentimental. I knew that as much as he wanted to see me married, when the time actually came, he would have misgivings." I didn't tell Lawrence that I thought it might also have had something to do with my father's hope of Eric and I forming an attachment instead. I could have been mistaken about that, anyway.

That evening in the drawing room after dinner, Lawrence and I made the announcement to the family. He stood beside the fireplace and beckoned me to join him, facing the rest of the household before us.

"Ladies and gentlemen," Lawrence said, with a bit of ridiculous grandeur, "there is something Charlotte and I wish to announce." All eyes were fixed on us, and every breath was held in anticipation, except, perhaps, for Eric's. "I have asked for her hand, and she has accepted."

His words lifted my heart, and I felt as if I were floating.

"Dear Charlotte!" exclaimed Mother, rising to embrace us. "How happy I am for you both!"

"You're getting married, Sister!" Mary Ann spoke in astonishment.

My father smiled sweetly at this picture of his family, but Mr. Kingsley's response was not as favorable as the rest. I don't think anyone else noticed, but as my mother

IN THE WAITING

had risen, so had Mr. Kingsley. He looked at me, but I saw no congratulations there. He slipped quietly from the room, and I returned to the enjoyment of sharing the excitement with my family.

"A spring wedding!" Mother had not stopped talking, "How perfect!" "Now, Mother…" I began, but Lawrence finished my thought.

"I'm sorry, Mrs. Devonshire, but I'm afraid we cannot yet set a date. The war still holds some uncertainty, so we may have to wait a little, though I am not sure how I will manage to do so." He looked at me and beamed.

∽

After everyone had retired for the night, Mary Ann knocked at my door.

I opened it and saw her grinning. "I was hoping for a little sister chat," she whispered. I rolled my eyes and smiled. "Very well."

She bounced onto my bed and beckoned me to join her. "So," she said, "how are you feeling? I bet you are even more excited than I."

"I am excited," I beamed. "I've dreamt of this for so long, and now that it is finally happening, I can hardly believe it."

Her face dimmed slightly. "Of course, I am happy for you, but I will miss having you down the hall."

"Oh, Mary Ann." I wrapped my arms around her and held her close. "I have not often told you just how much I value your friendship. I know I sometimes act like you annoy me, and granted, you do occasionally." We both giggled lightheartedly. "But I do love you. You are the best sister I could ask for."

We sat there for a moment, just soaking in the time we had.

I finally broke the silence. "I do not know how soon the wedding will be, but would you please be my maid of honor? I can't imagine taking this step without you by my side."

"Of course, I will! I would be honored!" She squeezed me again, and I laughed.

The next morning, I received more personal congratulations from Mother. She came to my room in much the same attitude as Mary Ann had displayed the night before.

"And what shall I get you to wear, miss?" Maggie was asking as she dug through the wardrobe.

"Oh, anything will do," I replied over my shoulder when I went to open the door. "Hello, Mother. Is there something you need?"

"No dear, I just wanted to congratulate you again on your engagement. The two of you make a fine pair, like I have always said. You have made your father and me very proud."

"Thank you, Mother." I let her hold me in a warm embrace—warmer, in fact, than any I had received from her in some time.

"Now then," she resumed with new vigor, though I was sure I saw traces of a tear on her cheek, "we must begin with the plans. Of course, we shall have the reception here. I shall need to create a list of improvements to be done beforehand. The draperies need cleaning or perhaps replacing. We shall need more chairs and tables for the dining room…"

"Mother! Please, do not get carried away. It is not as if we are the Barlows. I am sure Lawrence would not mind a small, simple wedding."

IN THE WAITING

She took my hands and looked seriously into my eyes. "My dear, it matters little what Lawrence prefers, and even less what you do. Weddings are the opportunities to show, or nearly determine, rank and sophistication. It is *I* who wishes to host a large and proper wedding, and so that is what will be done." She moved to the window and surveyed the park below. "It is quite cumbersome that the Lieutenant has refused to set a date."

"He is busy, Mother. You know that as well as I." My words attempted to show the delay did not bother me, but my tone held as much disappointment as my mother's. "I have asked Mary Ann to be my maid of honor."

"Excellent." She appeared to be planning something. "I am sure she will appreciate the chance to begin her own search for a husband when you are gone."

I had not been engaged more than a day, and already my mother was moving on to finding a match for Mary Ann. Well, perhaps it would help divert some of her controlling attention away from me for a while. So much the better.

"Later today you will join me in the parlor to discuss plans," she commanded rather than requested. But as a request would not have been optional anyway, I did not mind.

"Yes, Mother." I submitted. And so began the next stage of planning my wedding, since the first, securing a fiancé, was complete.

Chapter 18

Since the war continued to occupy much of Lawrence's time and did not really appear to have an end in sight, he decided we should further postpone the wedding until after things were more settled.

"I have nowhere yet for us to live, Charlotte. I'm afraid we must wait quite a while before we marry," he had said only a week or so after our engagement.

I understood and made no complaints, though I was disappointed. Still, so long as my future was secure, I was not in a hurry. Regardless of the uncertainty of the wedding day, we continued to make preparations. I enjoyed the special time it gave me with my mother and sister, and before I knew it, spring had turned to summer.

The warmer months brought a new vigor to the war as British General Henry Clinton launched another campaign up the Hudson River, and only a month later, Spain declared war on Great Britain. Lawrence was, of course, further preoccupied by his work as a result, so I kept myself busy with sewing, shopping, and planning.

"Shall we go shopping this afternoon, Charlotte?" Mary Ann inquired one morning at breakfast.

"I do hope you two have not spent all my money yet," Father noted teasingly.

"Oh, Father, you cannot expect Charlotte to marry an officer in rags, can you?" She tossed her head in mock disgust.

"Don't worry, dear," interjected Mother. "We may be in dismal financial straits, but Charlotte will get a respectable wedding if I have anything to say about it. I am just relieved she finally found a respectable man willing to take her."

I winced at the implication of her words but kept silent.

"May we invite Ellen and Lady Barlow to join us?" Mary Ann asked, ignoring the fact that I had yet to answer her first question.

"Yes, we may go shopping in town, and yes, you may invite Sarah and Ellen," I replied smiling, though I knew I would enjoy the outing less with Lady Barlow along.

Mary Ann rang the bell for Thomas and asked him to take a note to Fencomb.

Later that day, Mary Ann and I lighted the carriage for our ride to town. We had received a prompt reply from Penningcoll with regrets that neither guest would be joining us. Lady Barlow excused herself saying she was a married woman and not inclined to participate in the preparations for another woman's wedding. Ellen Barlow likely had a better reason but said only that she was otherwise engaged for the afternoon.

"'Tis a shame the Barlows could not come," Mary Ann remarked, bobbing up and down with the jostling of her seat, "though I do appreciate more time with you." She smiled, and I returned her look of sisterly love.

"I am not surprised that Lady Barlow declined, however," she continued. "She must be a little annoyed that you have proved to be a good catch and are enjoying the pleasures of a bride while she is suffering in her, dare

I say, limp marriage." She appeared rather satisfied with herself.

"Mary Ann! Don't say such things! She and Edward seem quite suited to one another." "Well, I can't see any sort of passion between them? Can you?"

"Marriage is not about passion; it is about responsibility to the future of one's family and the security of the children one expects."

Mary Ann studied me for a moment. "But I see the passion Lawrence has for you. You cannot tell me that that has not influenced your decision to accept him."

I blushed heavily, recalling again the kiss he and I had shared, as well as the many other tokens of affection he had shown me. "I do admit that it has not hindered my approval of the match," I replied carefully, "but I do believe I would have accepted him whether I felt anything for him or not. He is a gentleman and, moreover, a gentleman who can support me, and you, and Mother, when the need arises."

She was contemplating what I said, but thankfully did not press any further with questions.

༄

As I was no longer working with Eric at Penningcoll, I did not see him often, nor ever alone in the way I once had. Still, I saw even less of him than one would expect. In fact, it almost seemed as if Mr. Kingsley was avoiding me. I supposed that was for the best. After all, if I could be so shaken by only a few moments with him, it was probably a good thing there was distance between us.

Unfortunately, my separation from Mr. Kingsley did not cure all qualms and tensions I had in my relationship with Lawrence. Yes, Lawrence was as attentive as ever, even more so. Perhaps that was what bothered me. I was still getting used to being loved the way Lawrence loved me. One day, we were in the parlor together, Mary Ann was in the garden painting, Father was at Fencomb meeting with Andrew Barlow, and Mother had stepped out to discuss some household business with Mrs. Phillips. I was sitting in my usual place on the sofa, and he was on a chair opposite me, staring at me intensely.

"Mother suggests we serve veal at the reception. What do you think?" I looked down at my embroidery while awaiting a reply.

"It does not matter to me at all what is served at the reception. It is what happens after the reception that I care about." His eyes had not moved at all, but when I found in them nothing but sincerity, I blushed scarlet. He could not be implying what I thought he was. I mean, I had never been engaged before, but I could not imagine that such a phrase was entirely proper.

"Oh, yes," I answered shakily, "we will serve champagne in the ballroom after the meal." He did not say anything to that, but instead rose and joined me on the sofa.

"Charlotte," he spoke sweetly and gingerly reached for my hand. "Tell me again you love me. I fear I have only dreamt it."

"Of course I love you, Lawrence. Would I be marrying you if I didn't?"

He brushed his other hand against my neck and smiled broadly. "You make me the happiest man alive."

I smiled and closed my eyes. It was so wonderful to be so loved. I thanked God for this blessing and chided myself for being so ungrateful as to have ever questioned it.

His hand slid lower and caressed my shoulder. I squirmed uncomfortably, but he didn't seem to notice.

"Lawrence, please." He only moved closer. "I really should go see if Mother needs me," I said standing quickly, leaving him leaning over the spot where I had just been.

"Charlotte, you say you love me, but at times like these, you certainly don't act like it. If I had not received a positive reply to my proposal, I would think you do not desire my affection." He seemed hurt, but I was hurt myself by his apparent disregard for my comfort. He was not behaving like the gentleman he was.

"I am sorry, I just...I'm not used to being loved the way you love me. I am not sure how to act." I was rather sheepish. I was afraid of messing up our relationship by failing to handle affection the way a lady ought.

He grinned and stood. "I know, my dear, and I can be patient. You will have time to get used to it." He clasped and kissed my hand before I took my leave, no more and no less certain of my feelings and choices than before.

A couple days later, I received an unexpected letter that helped me answer some of my uncertainties.

"Charlotte," Father called to me from his study door when I was about to climb the stairs after a particularly enjoyable afternoon ride on Marble.

"Yes, Father?" I went to him.

"This came for you," and he handed me the envelope, but there was no return address or name on it.

"Thank you." I took it immediately to my room to discover who the sender could be.

Not long after I had situated myself on my settee and opened the letter, I found the sender to be none other than Bridgett Olsen. "Oh!" I exclaimed. "Dear Bridgett!" I hurried to read the rest.

IN THE WAITING

Charlotte,

I'm just writing to give you thanks again for your helping me and my family. You have a gift, and I am so pleased you have found a cause to use it for. We have not yet been discovered, but everyday since our flight from home, we have relied on good souls like you for our safety and provision. Father's leg has healed well, and he is walking fine.

Because you followed the path you have been called to, we are alive and well. You have a dear heart, and I pray to the good Lord that you never have to give up the purpose He has given you.

Your Grateful Friend, Bridgett

I sat in still silence for a moment, and with a sudden realization, I found myself shocked.

Bridgett was right. I did feel a sense of purpose when helping the Patriots. I didn't notice how much I actually cared about doing so until I stopped. Since my engagement I hadn't done anything at Penningcoll, and I believed that was why I was having such a hard time feeling settled with my decision to marry Lawrence. I knew that marrying him would mean I would be giving up my study of medicine and my opportunity to use what I had learned for a cause I cared about. Yes, I did care about the Patriot cause. It was another thing I was finally able to put into words. I was, by the general standard, a Patriot. I would have been more bothered by this admission if it was not overshadowed by the admission that I had felt a stronger sense of purpose fixing Mr. Milton's leg at Penningcoll than I did when I accepted Lawrence's proposal. All of this was just too much to take. I felt I didn't even know myself anymore. Finally, all the barriers I had put up to hide the truth from myself came crashing down. All it took was the reading of a simple note.

I pictured myself sitting in a stark parlor with an empty expression, Lawrence standing over me with his hands on my shoulders, and I shuttered. What a useless life that would be. But no, not useless. I would have children to raise. Yet that was even worse. I could see Lawrence as a husband, but not as a father.

I stopped myself there. Enough was enough. I was just letting fears and nerves get the better of me. Lawrence would make a fine father, and I a fine wife and mother. And again, though I could now concede to my patriotism, I did not see Lawrence as the enemy. He was only doing his duty. All would be well, and all would have to be well, for I had made my promise and would hold to it.

Once again, I made an effort to suppress my uneasiness and do what needed to be done. I said a quick prayer, asking God to give me the strength to give up what I must to marry the Lieutenant, and I began dressing for the evening meal.

When I was ready, I opened my door to find Eric on the other side about to knock. "Mr. Kingsley! You startled me."

"I'm sorry, Charlotte."

I cringed at his persistence to use my first name. "What do you want?" I asked coolly.

"I hate to ask this of you, and there is every chance this conversation is not necessary, but I felt I should let you know that we may have another guest soon." He leaned closer and whispered, "James Olsen."

"I see. Well, as I have said, I do not feel right about… entertaining a guest with the wedding approaching. I am sure you can manage without me." I felt almost cruel refusing my help that way, but I had just gone through all of that. I knew it would not make my task any easier if I were to reopen the brief chapter of my life called Penningcoll. I hoped Bridgett would forgive me for not being there to meet her husband, but I was sure she would understand if she knew my reasons.

Eric had waited for a moment after I had answered. Perhaps he was hoping I would change my mind, but when I didn't, he said, "Very well, Miss Devonshire. Shall we join your family downstairs?"

I nodded, but before we went to supper, I decided I should take the opportunity to tell him what he deserved to hear. "Wait," I said, glancing down the hall to make sure we would not be heard. "I have just received a note from Bridgett."

He gave me his full attention, "What did she say?"

"It does not matter, except it has made me realize a few very important things." I swallowed. "I am a Patriot," I whispered.

He grinned, "Well it's about time you admitted it. I've known for some time." When he saw in my eyes how much it had cost me to say what I did, he became more serious and added, "Thank you for telling me."

I smiled weakly, relieved to have been able to say it out loud. "But what does that mean for you and the Lieutenant?"

"I have to believe that if his circumstances were different, he would be a Patriot too.

Right now, he is doing what he must as an officer. As you said, the day will come when I can be honest with him, and he will understand."

"Then why do you not help at Penningcoll?"

"Believing what I do is one thing, but actively working against Lawrence is another." He did not reply, but turned, offering his arm, and together we went down.

Chapter 19

Contrary to my plan of permanent separation, Eric could not deal with Penningcoll's guest himself. I heard a light tapping on my door a few nights later. I thought perhaps it was Mary Ann, awakened by a dream or wanting to talk, but when I went to check, it was Mr. Kingsley's face I beheld in the flickering light of a candle. Looking down, I pulled my robe more tightly around me, embarrassingly conscious of the situation in which I found myself. He followed my gaze for a moment, but his eyes rose with mine, and a flush raised in his cheeks.

"Yes? What do you want?"

"Oh, sorry, yes." He seemed distracted and flustered. "It's James. He is very ill." "What do you think I can do about it?"

He took a step back in astonishment. "I should think you would wish to try anything you could for Bridgett's husband?"

"I'm sorry. You're right, it's just… give me a moment." I shut the door. When I opened it a few minutes later, I was dressed and ready to break the promise I had made to myself by returning to Penningcoll and actively participating in the Patriot cause.

We crept silently down the stairs and out the back door. There was no time to fetch Marble, so again we had to make do with only one horse. This time, however, Eric

IN THE WAITING

did hold me between his arms and took the reins himself. The night was chilly, and I had gained enough trust for this man that I did not mind. It was not the same to be near Eric as to be near Lawrence. With the Lieutenant, I could not anticipate his moves, but with Eric, I never considered the possibility of him doing something that would make me uncomfortable. I recalled the dance we had shared in Penningcoll months ago and realized how different I had felt then compared to how I had felt in the parlor a few days ago with my fiancé.

We reached the house without incident, and Eric lifted me easily from the saddle.

"I made a bed of blankets for him by the fire, but I did not know how else to help him."

The scene I faced when he opened the door was not an easy one to grasp. The room was depressingly dark, except for the small fire on the hearth. A mass of blankets and cloth lay in front, a red glow illuminating a pale face peeking through the folds. In the midst of the crackling of the fire, heavy, raspy breathing filled the air. Eric led me to the weak form, and we knelt on either side of him. A terrible fit of coughing overtook James Olsen. I had little idea what it was that ailed the man before me, but I knew that he was not well and that I had been called upon to save his life. I would do everything I could. I took a moment to sort through everything I knew about such illnesses and came up with little helpful information.

"Was this what he was like when he arrived?" I asked.

"He was coughing, and a bit pale, but he has gotten much worse since this morning." We looked each other in the eye. Eric sought to read my thoughts on James' condition, but I sought strength. Why I sought strength from him, I could not say, but I needed it from somewhere, and I thought he may be able to give it. He offered his hand, but I just stared at it. He did not insist, but drew it away, offering instead encouragement. "I know you will do what you can, and that is all anyone can ask. Just let me know what you need."

"Stoke the fire and boil some water," I commanded him. "I have heard of plasters being rubbed on the chest and stomach to help with coughs. I think the recipe I saw called for…what was it? Sweet almond oil and candle wax? Oh, I wish I had that book here."

"You do!" Eric jumped up. "Remember? You left in such a hurry last time you were here, you left a couple books behind."

"Really?" I remembered why I had left so abruptly, but I was surprised I had not noticed before now that the books were missing. In fact, come to think of it, I hadn't read any of my father's research books since Lawrence's proposal. I supposed I would have to get used to that, just as I had to get used to the Lieutenant's deepening affection.

Eric handed me the books, and I flipped through looking for the recipe I needed. "Here it is!" I exclaimed and showed him.

"Excellent! I will have to go back to Longford for these items. We do not have them here." He hesitated. "I am sorry, but will you be alright here on your own? Someone really should stay with him."

I half smiled at his concern. "I will be fine. It is James I am worried about." "I will hurry." And with that, he was gone.

James awoke an hour or so later and was alarmed to find a stranger next to him.

"Do not worry," I assured him. "I am here to help you. My name is Miss Devonshire, and I am a friend of Mr. Kingsley and of your wife."

He calmed down, but not before he had coughed

several times. "You know my Bridgett?"

"Yes," I said, replacing the blankets that had moved in his panic. "She was here many months ago before moving on to Connecticut."

He sighed. "What is today?" he inquired. It was no wonder that he was so disoriented. "It is past midnight, so it is July 4th."

"Do you realize today is the anniversary of the signing of the Declaration of Independence?" he asked weakly. He coughed again. "Bridgett and little Jimmy will be celebrating, I'm sure." He smiled, but I saw the tears in his eyes.

"You miss them very much."

"It would not be so bad if I knew for certain I would see them again soon, but half the time I am unsure of my own safety, and the rest of the time I fear for theirs. It is no way to live."

"Do you regret your commitment to the cause?" I asked, thinking of my own journey of uncertainty.

"Oh, no. As Mr. Paine says, 'We have the power to begin the world over again,' and I want to be a part of that. I want to ensure a safe, free, and worthwhile future for my son, and if that means I am not here to see him enjoy it, then so be it." He coughed a few more times.

"May I remove your shoes? It should make you more comfortable." He nodded.

"I am sorry we don't have a bed. The upstairs of the house was left empty." I worked to remove the boots, and as I did, a small slip of paper fell from the left one. "What is this?" I questioned.

He answered calmly, "It is a letter for General Washington." Then he began to panic once again. "I have to go! I'm late already!" he exclaimed, pushing the blankets away and grabbing the letter from me.

"Mr. Olsen! You are in no condition to stand, let alone travel across the sound to Fairfield!"

"No, no, I'm fine. I have to deliver this message." He tried to prop himself up but only fell back down again in a fit of coughing.

Eric rushed in at that moment, carrying several bottles and bags. "Here, I found all I could." He hurriedly dumped the load on the table.

I surveyed the pile and said, "This will do. Thank you," then got to work. "Mr. Kingsley," James called weakly.

Eric looked at me. I nodded, assuring him I could do this without his help, so he went to James' side. "Yes, Mr. Olsen?"

"This note must be delivered to General Washington. There is a house in Fairfield with deep blue curtains hanging in the lower windows and green on the top. From there, another courier will take it to Washington."

"Why do you tell me this? You will be well enough to take it in a week or so, I am sure." "It cannot wait that long."

Even with the distraction of mixing the plaster, I knew what James was asking Eric to do. "You want me to take it for you?"

"I would not ask you to risk so much, for you have already done so much for me, but this is a matter of urgency. Deliveries must be made on time, or the entire network is at risk. Timing is everything in this business."

"I understand." Eric looked at the paper in his hand, then at the young father who thought only of the country he wished to leave behind for his son. "I will do it."

My heart felt like it had stopped beating, and I was glad I was not in view of either of the men. It was just so dangerous. Penningcoll was different. It was a stationary and overlooked place. Traveling with evidence of one's

IN THE WAITING

traitorship was something far worse.

"Thank you," James said, in a voice much less strained. He had used what energy he had, and so fell asleep.

I brought the plaster over, but let Eric rub it into Mr. Olsen's skin. "Do you really mean to do it?" My voice was quiet.

"I must," he said, not looking up from his work.

"I know. You would not be the man I know you are if you were to refuse." He did look up then. "What is that man like? The one you think I am."

I chided myself for leading to such an inquisition, but I answered simply, "He is a gentleman." Though simple, the answer was not lost on him. He did not tease me for it, and I was grateful.

He changed the subject. "You have a gentleman of your own now." "So called." I said under my breath.

Eric's face turned to a look of worry. "Charlotte…" He waited until my eyes met his. "Has he done anything… ungentlemanly to you?"

"No, no, at least not really. We are engaged, after all." I shifted where I sat on the floor, trying to dispel the heavy air between us. He, however, sitting still and stiff, swallowed hard.

"You know, if you have changed your mind, it isn't too late to end the engagement. It would be better now than later." He watched closely for my reaction.

I wanted to be shocked, but I wasn't, so I just pretended. "What makes you think I have changed my mind? Furthermore, what would people say if I were to walk out on him now? I could not break my promise. It would completely ruin my reputation. Besides, it would hurt Lawrence too much."

"Does it not matter even more what God thinks?"

"Well, of course, but wouldn't He also want me to

keep my promise?"

"You said you would marry him. You have not said your marriage vows yet. God would not want you to commit your life to someone with whom you will not be safe."

"I did not say I feel unsafe with him!" I lashed. "You did not have to," replied Eric calmly.

I didn't know how to respond to that, so I ignored it. "I will be fine."

"Charlotte." He offered his hand again, but again I did not take it. "Fine is not good enough for a woman like you." His voice dropped to a whisper. "I want you to have a life filled with joy and love."

I looked down, heat rising to my cheeks. Why was it that Eric seemed to care so much about me? Lawrence cared about me, of course, but it was so different. It was almost as if... no, Eric didn't love me, did he?

"Come," he said, rising to his feet. "I need to get you back before the sun begins to rise.

James seems to be sleeping peacefully enough. Thank you for your help."

I was glad for the end of the conversation, and though I certainly was worried for Eric's task ahead, I thought perhaps it would not be a terrible thing for him to be removed from Longford for a few days. I needed to assure myself of the rightness of my intentions once again, and that could not happen if Mr. Kingsley was around trying to tear down every wall I had to rebuild.

Chapter 20

We rode back to the house, and I managed to get into bed unseen. Maggie did not wake at the usual time but instead let me sleep. When I asked her why she had let me miss breakfast, she replied saying, "You just looked too tired, Miss. Your eyes were puffy and your hair was a mess. It just looked like you'd barely gotten to sleep." I was sure she was right, for when I did finally rise, I did not look much better than her harsh description. I did not explain myself. I couldn't have done so honestly and so thought it better not to try.

Maggie helped make me more presentable, and then she remembered that my father had asked her to tell me to meet him in his study as soon as I was ready.

"I am sorry to have kept you waiting, Father," I said as I entered the room. "What is it you wanted to see me about?"

"Ah, Charlotte, come, have a seat." He gestured to one of the two cushioned chairs by the fireplace and, once I had sat, took the other. "I wanted to discuss with you your marriage to Lieutenant Taylor." His eyes searched me, and I knew this was going to be more than just a discussion about wedding details.

"He has assured me of his love for you, and I have no reason to doubt your love for him except… Let me cut to the chase. Do you love Lieutenant Taylor?"

I was taken a little off guard by the directness of the question. "I am ready to marry him.

And besides, what is there not to love, he is everything I have sought in a husband."

"You did not answer my question, and though I mean no disrespect to your fiancé, I thought perhaps…he might be making you uncomfortable at times? He *is* a gentleman, is he not?"

"Whatever would make you think otherwise?" As close as I was to my father, I was not about to divulge my apprehensive thoughts to him. He would be very disappointed in me if he knew how selfish I had been in my contemplations. I had a duty to my family and would fulfill it. There was no turning back now, and when I really thought about it, I saw there was no good reason to turn back anyway.

"I heard…never mind. If you are confident in your choice, I trust you. Just know that I love you very much. You have nothing to prove, and you need not do anything to earn my love." He rose and planted a kiss on my head.

"Thank you, Father." I smiled. "I love you too."

He crossed to the window. "I noticed that a couple of my medical books are missing from the library." He looked sideways at me. "Are you reading them again?"

"I've looked through them a bit."

He chuckled. "I remember when you were little, you used to sit on my lap and insist I read to you from whichever research book or encyclopedia I had nearest." His eyes held the light of sweet memories long past. "I never understood why you loved it so much."

"It was a way to spend time with you. It was a special pastime we had just the two of us, and I suppose the more you read, the more I valued what you read in addition to your company."

IN THE WAITING

"Whatever the reason, I thank God for that time we had. And I am sorry we have not continued the practice, especially as you will not be at Longford much longer." The tears began to fill his eyes, encouraging mine to do the same. "But," he continued, "no matter where you go or with whom I share you, you will always be my daughter."

I stood then and came to embrace him. "Oh, Father." The tears flowed freely. It would be hard to leave, but it was the natural order of things and my duty to do so. My father knew that as well as I.

"Alright," Father said, taking a deep breath, "that's enough of that. Your mother will be wondering where you are. She was concerned when Maggie told us you would not be coming to breakfast. You had better go find her."

"Thank you, Father, for everything."

When I stepped out of the study, Mr. Kingsley was there, apparently waiting for me. I quickly wiped the remaining tears from my face.

"I wanted to let you know that Mr. Olsen is doing much better this morning."

"Oh, that's wonderful! I am so glad he will be with his family again soon." I whispered to match the level of his voice. Who knew when someone might walk by? Raising my voice to a normal level, I continued, "Might I ask if you have heard yet when your own family will be back? It has been several months. You must miss them."

"This is a change." He smiled. "You have never been concerned about my loneliness before. Why the sudden interest?"

I raised an eyebrow in reply and waited for him to give an answer.

"As a matter of fact, my parents have decided that there is no use waiting for the end of the war. They are due to arrive in the colonies within the next few days."

"Does this mean you will be going home soon?" I was surprised to discover this possibility actually disappointed me.

"Let us take one day at a time." He looked down at the three-cornered hat he held in his hands. "I also came to tell you goodbye."

I swallowed my worry, took a deep breath, and replied simply, "Be careful; I wish you luck."

"I hope I have not offended you in any way, Miss Devonshire, or overstepped at all. You do know I only want what is best for you, as your friend."

"You have been much better to me than deserved, I am sure. I shudder to think how I treated you in your first weeks here." I blushed in embarrassment.

He grinned and chuckled softly. "You treated me better than I did you."

"What are you going to tell my father? Won't he miss you?" I asked, returning to the subject at hand.

"Don't worry. I'll think of something."

"Then I shall see you when you return," I said lightly, offering my hand to shake.

He nodded, tightening his jaw in his familiar way, and took my hand. But instead of shaking it, he bowed and kissed it lightly.

"Farewell, Charlotte."

My heart fluttered, but I managed to reply evenly, "May God be with you."

Chapter 21

That afternoon, Mary Ann and I decided to go for a walk. While out, we passed near Fencomb and thought it might be nice to stop briefly to say hello to the ladies there. It had been some time since we had seen Ellen and Lady and Mrs. Barlow.

"Let's visit Fencomb; Charlotte, can we please?" Mary Ann had said. "Without an invitation?"

"We don't need an invitation to see Ellen," she assured me. "It is not a formal visit."

I smiled. "All right then, as you wish. We could tell her about the wares we've bought for the wedding, and Sarah too, if she could be bothered with it." I rolled my eyes. I did not actually care very much about Lady Barlow's attitude towards me. I understood that our childhood friendship was only that, and that the relationship we had now was purely neighborly, and not particularly friendly. I understood why as well. A lady such as she would demean herself by being too closely acquainted with an unmarried woman of slipping rank like me. I did not blame her.

We marched up the gravel drive to the grand house and rang. The butler let us in, and as we entered the foyer, memories of the Thanksgiving ball came to me. I blushed in recollection of Ada Winters on the arm of Mr. Kingsley, at my doing no less.

We were led to the parlor, and he announced us. We walked into a rather awkward scene. Mrs. Barlow had stood from her chair. Sarah rotated in her seat and looked at us with wide eyes. Ellen, who was sitting on the couch drinking tea, began choking and coughing. All this was odd, but I hardly noticed any of it, for standing beside Ellen was none other than Lieutenant Taylor.

"Welcome, girls!" Mrs. Barlow hastened to say, as she did not seem to find the situation as uncomfortable as her daughter and daughter-in-law obviously did. "How good of you to drop by. Join us, please! Ellen and the Lieutenant were just recalling some stories of their time in New York last year. Ellen intends to return in the autumn, you know."

"Ah! How very nice," I said with a smile more confident than I felt. As he was coming to greet me, I could not find a reason for Lawrence to be here, but he must have one.

"Miss Devonshire, Miss Mary Ann! How wonderful to see you both, though it has not been terribly long." He winked at me. I blushed, though no one else but perhaps Mary Ann saw.

"I would not have expected to see you here," Mary Ann noted incredulously.

"Oh, I was here to discuss some business with Sir Edward, but with that done, I found the company in here too enjoyable to leave just yet." He looked glowingly around the room. It seemed his eyes stayed a little longer on Ellen than the others, but I was sure I was imagining things.

"Ellen, we wanted to tell you about some plans for the wedding." Mary Ann seemed satisfied with his explanation, as I was. "Do you have a few moments to perhaps go out to the garden with us?"

"I'm not sure," she replied with disinterest. "I have a

few things I really should be getting to." She stood and so did Sarah.

"Yes, you must excuse us," Lady Barlow added. "We have spent long enough visiting today."

"Oh, but..." Mrs. Barlow was cut off by a look from Lady Barlow.

"I understand," I answered with a smile. "Perhaps some other time. I am sorry to have come on you unannounced."

"Do come back soon," entreated Mrs. Barlow.

"We shall." I squeezed her hand in gratitude for her sweet and generous nature. "And I shall take my leave as well," Lawrence announced. "Thank you for your fine hospitality, ladies." He bowed, and the three of us exited.

"Would you like me to walk back to Longford with you?" asked Lawrence when we had come outside.

I smiled, appreciating his gentlemanly concern for us. "I would like that," I answered. We walked quietly for a time.

"What about the wedding were you going to tell Ellen?" he inquired. "May I hear it? It is my wedding too, after all." He slid his hand around mine and grinned down at me.

I blushed. "Of course you can."

"I think I'll walk a bit ahead, if you don't mind," interrupted Mary Ann. She smiled and raised an eyebrow at me.

Lawrence took advantage of our new solitude and lifted my hand to his lips. "Now, about these plans."

"Ah, yes. Well, I told you Mother's ideas for the reception." He nodded. "We have picked out lovely pink material for Mary Ann's dress..."

"What is it you will be wearing?"

Again, I blushed. "It's supposed to be a surprise," I

admonished teasingly. "Humor me," he said.

"Fine. It is the palest cream silk, with lots of lace."

He stopped walking, causing me to halt as well. "And is there a ribbon here?" He traced my waist with fingers.

"No," I replied with a shaky voice.

He got the hint. "I'm sorry, Charlotte. I should not rush you." He took my hand again and we continued on our way. Mary Ann was now quite far ahead of us, and we had not much longer to walk before reaching Longford.

"Speaking of rushing," I began, "I do not mean to do so now, but do you know yet when we might be able to set a date? We need to talk to the minister soon."

He let go of my hand and, lifting his hat, brushed his over his hair. "Well, not really. I am sorry, but you know how unsure everything is these days. I need to secure a home for you first. You understand?"

"Certainly." I smiled sweetly at him. It was nice to have someone with whom I was planning a future. "Have you made any progress?"

"I heard there is an empty estate behind Longford. Penningcoll, I think it is called." My knees nearly gave out, and I stumbled.

"Are you alright?" he asked, reaching out to steady me.

"Yes, yes. I must have stepped on something. Pe... Penningcoll, you said?"

"Yes, though I have had a very difficult time finding the owner. All I have been able to discover is that it is supposed to belong to some crazy old man. Anyway, I am still figuring out the legal aspect of trying to acquire it. Then, of course, it will need some work before it is ready to be lived in…"

"I understand. I thank you for taking such care in preparing our life together." He grinned.

IN THE WAITING

We stopped on the front steps of Longford. Mary Ann must have already gone inside. "Of course, Charlotte. And I hope you know how much it pains me to wait so long to have you as my own dear wife."

I nodded. "Won't you come in?" I invited.

"I think not, I ought to get back to town. I am still an officer on duty." He bowed. "What a hardworking gentleman you are." I smiled.

He stood a little taller. "For you, I would be anything." My heart leapt, he turned away, and I closed the door.

༽

On a particularly warm night, several days later, I decided to go up to the widow's walk for a while. With my marriage coming quickly, or at least coming, and Eric still not back from Fairfield, I needed some time alone to think. I looked out across the bay. Port Jefferson seemed to be in quite a bustle. A few British ships had just come in, and I could see dozens of soldiers scurrying about like ants on the shore and on the decks. I wondered what was going on, but it was not terribly uncommon for there to be such excitement when new troops arrived. I thought of Lawrence and was curious what he might be doing down there, if he was involved at all. It felt rather special to be engaged to a man so admired and needed, even though I would have rather had him fight for the other side of the war.

He had been especially busy since he escorted me home from Fencomb, and I had only seen him one time since. I breathed in the crisp night air and reminisced about the afternoon before, when he had taken me for a picnic in the orchard. It had been quite a surprise, but a welcome one. He had a blanket and a large basket of delicacies brought out for us, and we sat together under the shade of the trees.

"You have such a glow about you, Charlotte," he had commented. I blushed. "Only when you are here," I replied.

He smiled and moved closer. He picked an apple from above us and started to slice it with a knife. "Here," he said, bringing a juicy piece to my mouth.

I bit into the sweet fruit, and he watched me with delight from his reclined position. "Tell me," I began when I had swallowed. "What is it about our marriage to which you are most looking forward?"

"Well," he answered, sitting up, "when we are married, I can do this all I want." He leaned forward, put his hand behind my neck, and kissed me.

A surge of energy had rushed through me.

"You must love me a great deal to desire such things," I replied with my eyes downcast and my cheeks flaming once he had released me. "I am so grateful that you took notice of me."

"And you must love me a great deal to flatter me as you do." He grinned.

The rest of our picnic was peaceful and as pleasant as any time should be with one's fiancé.

More shouting brought me back to my place on the widow's walk. I took a deep breath and closed my eyes. I let the wind loosen my hair. Above the far-off shouts and sounds of the port, I could hear the chirp of crickets and the splashing of waves. I had peace for only a moment. For days I had been anxious, not only about Eric's danger, but also about Lawrence's plans for our home. The sweet times we had in each other's presence could only do so much to quell my worries and concerns about what I still dreamed would be a wonderful and sure life. Penningcoll would be a wonderful spot, no doubt, but I hoped that

IN THE WAITING

Eric would return in enough time to vacate the estate and make alternative arrangements before the Lieutenant discovered what had been going on there.

Already I was giving up that which I had learned to love. Such is the nature of marriage.

It is a duty that comes at a price. I hoped a good marriage based on love would come with benefits to soothe the loss. I sighed, supposing I would soon find out.

Chapter 22

The next day at tea time, Lawrence was able to join my family in the parlor. We opened the large windows to enjoy a bit of a breeze on that hot Saturday morning. Father took up his newspaper, Mary Ann started on a painting, Mother continued her needlepoint, and the Lieutenant and I each chose a book from those lying on the side table and desk. We all remained preoccupied with our own activities until a gasp issued forth from my father.

"Whatever is the matter, dear?" inquired Mother. When no response came, for he seemed stunned into silence, she rose and took the newspaper from where it had fallen into his lap and began to read aloud.

> General William Tryon, former royal governor of New York, and 2,600 Loyalists and British regulars on forty-eight ships raided Fairfield, Connecticut on July 7-8, burning the city to the ground in response to Patriot defiance. It was known that spy activity was prevalent there. The British army believes this will halt such operations. This is a day of celebration

IN THE WAITING

```
for all those subjects loyal to
the King.
```

I gasped and sank back in my seat. *Eric, what about Eric?* was all I could think. "Burned? The whole city? Burned?" Mary Ann was incredulous. She had always seen the world as better than it was, and living on Long Island at this time helped shield her from the truths of the war around her.

"Such a shame," Lawrence said, taking a sip of tea. "But then they knew what the consequences of their actions would be."

"Indeed," remarked Mother softly. I was unsure to which comment she was responding. My father, more than anyone, seemed deeply disturbed at this news, and said nothing.

Though I knew he would not have shared with Father *why* he had gone, I wondered if Eric had told him *where* he had gone. Though, if he had, why would my father not have said as much in his explanation for his obvious discomfort at the news?

All this was very alarming, but two questions continued to roll over and over in my mind: Where was Eric, and was he okay?

☙

I went to Penningcoll early the next morning and found Mr. Olsen much improved. I gave him the rest of the poultice to apply himself and resupplied his food and water.

"Thank you again, Miss Devonshire, for all you have done for me. I will be well enough to travel soon. If I do not see you again, I want you to know how much I appreciate your efforts for our common cause."

I nodded, bade goodbye, and left for Longford for breakfast. At the meal, my father was brought a letter marked urgent.

"Thank you, Thomas." He wiped his mouth and opened the letter, reading it quickly with grave eyes. "Charlotte, would you please see me in my study after the meal?" He folded the letter and tucked it into his coat pocket.

"Certainly, Father." My heart quickened. What could be in the letter that he would share with me and not with Mother or Mary Ann?

As soon as my father had shut the door behind us in his study, he removed the letter from his pocket. From inside the envelope, he drew out a second letter and handed it to me. *Charlotte* was written in a shaky hand on the back of the folded piece of paper. I looked up at my father inquisitively.

"It is from Mr. Kingsley," he said matter of factly, but his face told me this was no usual correspondence. "I had better return to your mother. Take all the time you need." He closed the door on his way out.

I stared for several minutes at my name and paced the floor, wondering again what could have happened to Eric, and what he would need to tell me in a letter rather than in person.

Carefully, I unfolded the note, and began to read.

My Dear Charlotte,

I am sure you have heard by now the news of the atrocities done in Fairfield, though I doubt you have heard of them in as great of detail as I have experienced them. I am writing this from my cell aboard a British ship. I do not know which. I have been allowed one letter to my employer, your father of course, and have enclosed

IN THE WAITING

this note to you with some explanation.

First, I wish to say that I have failed the Patriots, I have failed James Olsen, and I have failed you. Though I was able to deliver the message, I was apprehended and have been charged with treason and espionage against the crown. I suppose I may as well take the time to tell you how this came to be.

After delivering the note, I decided to remain in Fairfield another day or two, as I had been invited to stay with the family of a man I met on the boat, and I had not yet found Mr. Milton, which I had hoped to do. On July 7th, the town received a warning from the fort at Black Rock Harbor that the British fleet was coming to take over. In a desperate attempt to protect the fort, many of the Patriots destroyed the Ash Bridge and kept the British from their initial plans. Unfortunately, their subsequent plans proved worse in many respects.

They started burning houses on the way back to their ships. Some of the men took up arms and attempted to fight for their homes, but success was not to be ours. And in fact, our attempts only aroused the British all the more. The next day, when German reinforcements arrived, fire after fire was lit. And before I knew it, the whole town was aflame.

I was in the home of that Patriot family when the screaming began. It happened so fast there was nothing I could do. I ran out into the street and black smoke filled my nostrils. Redcoats came from everywhere. I tried to wrestle the torch from a German soldier who came towards the house where I had been given shelter, but I was overpowered by several others and watched helplessly as mother and child were separated in the chaos. The visions of suffering I witnessed as I was driven through the streets with a small number of captured men were too terrible to describe. One by one the men turned from shouting with anger to crying pitiably as we passed piles of rubble that used to be their homes and the homes of their neighbors.

There is not much more to say on that account. I await the carrying out of my sentencing. I am sure you can guess what my punishment will be. All I hope and pray is that they never find out what part you played. As grateful as I am for the help you have given me and for the time we enjoyed together, I could never forgive myself if anything were to happen to you because of me. Promise me you will not do anything to risk being discovered.

I know this must be hard for you to read. Even though I know I am not particularly dear to you, I ask you not to weep for me, Charlotte, for I am going home to be with my true Father. I shall see you again someday. Until then, I must make sure you know that I go to my grave with a love for you so deep that even the entire British army in their attempts to crush my spirit cannot succeed in robbing me of this solace. As God goes with me, so also I know He goes with you. Live well the life with which He has blessed you.

Yours Always, Eric

I realized then that I had been holding my breath as I was reading, for at the letter's conclusion my gasps for air were almost uncontrollable as I tried to hold back my tears. I dropped to my knees on the hearth and let the grief, confusion, and regret overtake me. He loved me? I had suspected some level of fondness perhaps, some teasing interest, but not love. He had not shown me his love in any way like Lawrence always did. Why had he kept his love from me? But I already knew the answer. I knew it was because he was too much of a gentleman to interfere with my plans with Lawrence only for his own desires. Oh, why? Why would such a thing happen to such a good man? And he *was* a good man. I knew that now more than ever. No matter what his appearance, no matter what society thought of him, he was a man worthy of honor, for he was willing to sacrifice everything, his life, his desires, to fight for freedom as God had called him to.

In my stubbornness and pride, I had missed my chance to tell him what I really thought of him, and now he would never hear that I… that I loved him too. I gasped and wiped my tears in surprise. I loved him? No, how could that be? I was engaged to another man. A man of valor and prestige. A man any woman would desire. Yet, at the same time, this revelation made so much sense. Who had cared for me selflessly? Who had told me what I needed, and not what I wanted to hear? Who had guided me to become the woman I knew God designed me to be? It was not Lawrence. But what was I going to do about it? I was to marry the Lieutenant, and Eric would surely be executed. There was nothing I could do.

Or was there? What was stopping me from going and at least visiting? And couldn't Father pull strings to get him off with a warning? Perhaps there was not much evidence against him. But would Father do this if he knew the truth of Eric's doings? And what if my involvement were to come out? That would certainly seal Mr. Kingsley's fate. There was also the problem of not knowing exactly where he was. The surplus of ships had left Port Jefferson.

I did not have long to contemplate what actions were available to me before events started unfurling on their own. By that afternoon, lists of those arrested or killed had been posted, and all of our friends and acquaintances knew of Eric's arrest. Lady Barlow and Ellen wasted no time in coming to give us their condolences on the unfortunate connection we had in Mr. Kingsley.

"Such a shame," Sarah said. "Your father will have to work very hard to recover from this, you know. Such a bad connection is not easily forgotten by the public. He will need to make his position in opposition to Mr. Kingsley known right away."

"I am sure there is some misunderstanding," Mary Ann assured us all, though she did not sound particularly sure. "There is no way Mr. Kingsley is anything less than honorable."

"Well, you didn't see him at the autumn dance with Ada Winters," Ellen chimed in knowingly. "You may not have thought so highly of him if you had." She raised her eyebrows in superiority.

I squirmed under the false accusation of rakish behavior on the part of Mr. Kingsley. I knew better, but if I told them I did, they might grow suspicious as to how I knew and why I would defend him.

"Perhaps he was simply at the wrong place at the wrong time," I said, ignoring the comment rather than responding to it. "Regardless, I am sure my father will do what needs to be done in regards to Mr. Kingsley's welfare and our relationship to him."

Not only did we face a visit from the Barlow sisters, but Father also received a letter from Eric's parents that he felt he should share with us. They had returned to the colonies in time to hear of their son's arrest. They wanted Father to know that they blamed him and our family for Eric's downfall to the side of the enemy, and that they would be revoking his inheritance.

"Surely his beliefs are not recently formed," I said to Father once Mary Ann and Mother had left the room in quite a fearful tizzy over being so blamed. "They must have seen some of who he was becoming before they left for England."

"I am afraid they did, my dear. It was for that reason Eric was not invited to join them." He looked up at me with sad eyes that said more than his words.

The pieces began to fall into place in my mind. "You mean he did not stay behind because you asked him to work for you, but that you asked him to work for you because he had stayed behind?"

He nodded. "His parents agreed it would be best, believing I might be able to save him from his rebelliousness."

And I had done the opposite of help. I had enabled his rejection of his family. How could I have been so blind?

༄

I lay in bed that night feeling responsible for the entire situation. Yes, Eric was his own man, but I could have tried to prevent him from going to Fairfield at least. I could not sleep knowing that Eric's life was in danger and that I was in part to blame and had certainly shared in the crime. I would not promise what he had asked me to. I simply could not.

I sat up. I knew what I had to do. I hurriedly dressed in a simple dark dress and stole downstairs with a shawl, hat, and small purse in hand. I wrote a brief note and left it in my father's study for him to find in the morning. Brief though it was, I did my best to explain in full what I was guilty of doing over the past many months. Where I was going, there would be no point in hiding from the truth, and so I desired to reveal all to my father myself. He deserved that from me.

I did not want to risk being heard or seen, so instead

of going for Marble, I decided to walk down to the port. I found a small whale boat docked there and paid handsomely for the captain to take me aboard. I was going to Fairfield.

Chapter 23

Smoke still hung in the air as we reached the hidden cove where I disembarked. "Are you sure you'll be alright on yer own, miss?" the Captain asked.

"Yes, quite sure." I was resolute in my mission and was not about to let fear or anything else stand in my way. "You may return to your boat and go about your business."

He seemed doubtful, but shrugged his shoulders and did as I wished.

I walked along the muddy shore until a path opened to a road that seemed to lead to town. I followed the road, but in place of a town stood rows upon rows of blackened stone and charred wood piled where buildings used to be. Evidence of what had been was all around. Broken lanterns, ruined furniture, and singed clothing were strewn about the streets. The article Mother had read played back in my mind: ninety-seven homes, sixty-six bars, thirty stores and shops, three meeting houses, two schoolhouses, one jail, and one courthouse. How could the British army do something like this to an entire town? I didn't want to believe that Lawrence had anything to do with this act, just as he must have exaggerated the role he played in the hanging of the poor man in Setauket and could not have been aware of what had happened to Bridgett and her family.

Bridgett! I had not yet thought about her! Where was

she? Was she alright? Though it was the middle of the night, there were small groups of people digging through the rubble. They had nowhere else to go, and all were silent from the terrors they had witnessed. I began paying attention to their faces, hoping I would find her or Mr. Milton, unlikely as it was in a town this size, or at least what used to be a town this size.

"Miss Devonshire? Is that you?" I looked around trying to determine from whence the voice had come. "It is you!"

I saw at once that it was indeed Bridgett coming towards me, and I was glad to see her. "Bridgett! Are you alright? How is young James and your father?"

"They are fine. We are all fine. Shaken up to be sure, but we are alive and had little to lose in the fires anyway. We will start afresh again. They may destroy our homes, but they can't destroy our hope."

I smiled. Only Bridgett could have such an attitude when all around her was destruction. "But what are you doing here?" she asked, realizing how out of place I was.

I stood a little taller, and my smile disappeared. "I came to join in Mr. Kingsley's fate." "What? What has happened to kind Mr. Kingsley?"

I told her of his taking over her husband's mission, and that he had been taken during the fires.

"My James is in Setauket?" Her voice held both excitement and fear. "We haven't heard from him in weeks."

I looked around, saw a large, flat rock, and led her to sit down with me. "Yes, at least he was when I last saw him. He was doing quite well." She sighed in relief, and I continued, "Do you know where I will find the prisoners?" I asked.

"Well, I believe all the ships left once the damage was

done, but I suppose there might still be one with prisoners aboard."

"Thank you, Bridgett. I will do what I must to find Eric."

She reached out and squeezed my hand. "I will not try to convince you not to go. I can see in your eyes it would do no good, but I want you to be sure of what you are doing. What is said cannot be unsaid. You have a family and a fiancé to think about in addition to your friendship and involvement with Mr. Kingsley."

"I know, but doing what is right is more important than what my family or the Lieutenant thinks of me. It is you and Mr. Kingsley who taught me that, and I cannot ignore it, even if it means destroying my reputation and risking my life." I fingered my purse. "Besides, after all that has happened, and what Eric revealed to me in his letter, I am not sure where things stand between Lawrence and me anyway."

She reached out to still my hands. "I understand." She sighed and sat up straighter. "I really do wish I could help you, after all you have done for us, but I must find some food and get back to my father and son."

We rose from our makeshift bench.

"You have encouraged me, Bridgett, and that is what I needed most." I smiled. "I wish you the very best."

"Perhaps the next time we meet will be under better circumstances," she said hopefully. "Perhaps," I agreed, and we parted, each with tears in our eyes.

༶

By the breaking of dawn, tired though I was, I was closer to my planned destination.

After walking through the streets, asking everyone willing to listen where the British ships had gone, I had finally discovered that they had moved along the coast to Norwalk and had just looted and burned the village the previous day.

I knew that I was in desperate need of rest, but there was really nowhere to do so. I started down the road in the direction of Norwalk, hoping someone would pass me who could give me a ride. Before long, a farmer with a wagon carrying a small pile of salvaged but black belongings came along, and without much hassle, I convinced him to let me pay him to take me to the shore of Norwalk. I laid down on the small bit of empty space in the wagon and somehow managed to sleep during our all-too-short journey.

When we arrived, I was even more dirty, disheveled, and disoriented, but I was no less determined. I had planned to turn myself in before seeing Mr. Kingsley if that was necessary, for I was sure I would not be allowed into the brig otherwise. Besides, I did not even know aboard which ship he was being held.

I walked along the dock and joined the silence that hung in the air along with the mixture of smoke and fog. As I approached the nearest ship, I saw a form on the deck waving me down. He called to me, rather harshly.

"You there!" he shouted again. I looked around and saw no one else to whom he could be referring. "It's about time you showed up. We were told you'd be here an hour ago. Hurry up here now." He gestured for me to come aboard.

Though very confused, I thought it best to comply and so started up the plank.

"General Tryon likes a clean ship. You'll find all the laundry in bags past the brig. Don't mind that rebel scum down there, just stay outta reach from the cell and you'll be fine." He grinned, showing yellowed and crooked teeth.

IN THE WAITING

I didn't correct the misunderstanding, though perhaps for honesty's sake I should have. I supposed I looked the part of a maid. I simply followed him to the opening on the deck that led below and, when he had pointed and left, took the first step down the ladder.

"Just make sure you have it cleaned up quick and bring back the laundry in a few hours," he called over his shoulder.

I didn't understand how anyone could expect a person to clean laundry when almost every building for miles was burned to the ground, but that was not my current problem. I paused a moment before descending to the hold and took a deep breath. I was relieved to see there were no guards below, only the prisoners—or rather, prisoner. Only one was there, sitting on the floor against the bars, with his back to me. My eyes were still adjusting to the dark, and it took me a moment before I recognized the dejected form as that of Mr. Kingsley.

I rushed to him. "Eric!" I exclaimed when I was close enough that I could speak quietly without letting the soldiers above hear. Tears of exhaustion and relief ran down my cheeks.

He lifted his head in astonished bewilderment. "Miss Devonshire!"

Chapter 24

"What in the world are you doing here?" He stood hastily and rather unsteadily.

I wiped my tears and tried to catch my breath. "I could not just let them kill you. I am just as guilty as you, and you can't face this fate alone."

His brow furrowed. "You cannot mean what I fear you do."

I nodded, and sadness softened his expression. We both slid against the bars that separated us and sat on the floor facing each other.

"Charlotte," he whispered, "you can't." His hands grasped the cold metal, his knuckles white.

"Of course, I can!" Though his voice had not been commanding, my stubbornness still rose in opposition to his.

"No, you don't understand."

I tilted my head in questioning confusion.

"You can't because… I don't know what I would do if anything happened to you." His hand slid down the bar to meet mine. A pulse of warmth traveled through me in that instant. His eyes met mine and he said quietly, but confidently, "I love you."

Tears threatened to burst forth. "Oh, Eric," I began, "how did I not see it before?" I took a deep breath and listened for a moment for sounds of activity above. I heard nothing alarming. "When I read your letter, so much became clear to me, one revelation being how good you have been to me."

"But I have not been," he interjected earnestly. "What gentleman would tell a woman who is engaged to another man that he loves her? I was selfish to have told you what I did in that letter, and though I convinced myself it would keep you from doing anything rash, it has done the opposite."

"Eric," I said softly and surely, "first, with all that has happened these last many months, which I can see in clarity now, I cannot marry Lieutenant Taylor, even though I am sure he is my last chance for a respectable and fortunate marriage. It simply would not be right to marry a man I can no longer love."

His face showed some mixture of surprise and pride, and perhaps a glimmer of hope. "And second," I continued, "your letter said exactly what I needed to hear and no one, not even you, could have kept me from coming to you now."

His gray eyes glistened in the dim light. "You really are spectacular." He grinned and I blushed under his gaze.

"I am only trying my best to follow in your example and do what God requires. It is yourself with whom you should be satisfied. You have found your purpose in helping with the cause of liberty."

"Thank you, but you're mistaken. My purpose is not to secure liberty for all. I couldn't do it if I tried. My sole purpose is to love and serve God. I attempt to do this in a small way by helping the innocent and protecting the freedoms God gave to everyone."

Every time he spoke, I found new reasons to admire him.

"I did not understand this before as clearly as I do

now," he continued. "In fact, it was another visitor I had while the ships were docked in Port Jefferson who helped me see why I was willing to sacrifice what I have."

"Visitor?" I asked. "What visitor?"

He hesitated for a moment. "I suppose it would not hurt to tell you now." "Do you mean I know him?"

"The visitor was the one who gave us that cart of supplies we were unloading when you hurt your hand. And he has done much more to help than that as well. He is Mr. Andrew Barlow."

"Really?" I couldn't believe it. "A Barlow, a Patriot?" I had gathered that, as a soon-to-be minister, Mr. Barlow was not as ravenously in favor of the British cause as his younger brother, Sir Edward. Nevertheless, this was quite a shocking revelation.

I noticed after a moment of quiet that Eric's hand was still on mine, and the realization brought me comfort. I was still exhausted and now ragged with emotion. His familiar, yet somehow novel presence gave me strength.

"Charlotte," he began cautiously, "you really must be going. If they discover you know me, there will be no going back to your old life."

"I do not intend to go back to my old life, or haven't you been listening?" I said earnestly. "I am willing to risk exactly what you are."

"That doesn't mean you have to throw yourself at their mercy when you have not been caught. I doubt they would kill you, as they likely will me, but you most certainly would be imprisoned for a time and then ostracized."

"I do not care. I cannot care about what other people will think of me or what this will mean for my chances of marriage when I care so much more about standing up for what is right. I will not shrink from admitting that I believe the British are gravely in the wrong. If my voice and my story inspire others to stand up as yours has inspired me, then perhaps all is not lost. If nothing comes of it but my own growth of character as a woman who values truth and freedom, then that will be enough."

Our argument kept us distracted for a moment, and so we did not notice until it was too late that a soldier was descending the ladder.

"I told you not to mind him." His scolding was half-hearted. It was clear he had not heard the content of our conversation. His attention was not on me for long. "Get up, scum!" he commanded Eric angrily. He jingled with some keys.

I had moved to the laundry bags in the back, trying to determine if this was the moment of confession, or if I had better wait for the general to return.

But before I had made up my mind, he began unlocking the door of the cell. Eric was rightfully untrusting.

"What is this?" he asked firmly. "What are you going to do to me?"

"Gotta set you free," the soldier replied. It was clear he was not enjoying this task. "Set me free?"

"Yeah, turns out some high and mighty men from the island have convinced the general of your innocence." He added scoffingly under his breath, "Musta been some wealthy men."

I was beyond confused, even more so when he told *both* of us to follow him. Eric gave me a look of assurance and offered his hand to help me up the ladder, so I complied.

When he had led us off the ship, the soldier gestured to a rich but smoke-covered coach about a hundred yards off in the shade of some trees, then he turned and left. Two gentlemen were sitting inside waiting for us. As we approached the coach, my heart nearly stopped. The first I recognized as Mr. Barlow, which was not quite as shocking as it would have been only ten minutes earlier, but the second was on whose face my eyes remained frozen.

It was none other than Mr. Devonshire himself, my father.

"Father!" I began smoothing my hair and wiping my face. "What in the world are you doing here? How did you find me?"

"You did tell me in your note where you were going." His eyes moved to Mr. Kingsley and some silent message was sent, for it was Eric who spoke next.

"Miss Devonshire, I would like you to meet my informer, commander, and employer in *all* the work I, or should I say we, have done." "Father? You knew? This whole time?"

Opening the coach door, he took my hand to help me aboard as Eric followed. After instructing the driver to take us to Black Rock Harbor, he turned to me, tears filling his eyes. He swallowed hard and begged, "Can you ever forgive me for keeping it from you?"

"Of course!" I was too relieved to find Eric free to feel any offense. "Can you forgive me for the secrets I've kept from you?"

He smiled appreciatively and nodded.

Eric interrupted sheepishly, "And can you forgive me for keeping it a secret as well?"

"I know you did what you had to to protect us all," I assured him.

The look we exchanged spoke volumes to just how much had changed between us since our first meeting, and I smiled in spite of the strain of the last few days.

"Speaking of," said Eric, turning to Father and Mr. Barlow who sat across from us, "however did you manage to get me out of there?" he asked.

"Oh, it took some persuading to be sure, but thankfully

IN THE WAITING

the general was not aware of the extent to which you have aided his enemies." Mr. Barlow smiled broadly. "He had little with which to implicate you."

"I should let you both know," Father added, "that on our way here we were able to safely escort Mr. Olsen from Penningcoll to his family in Fairfield."

"Wait..." I was beginning to find that with every bit of added information I had even more questions. "What about Penningcoll? How is it that we could use the house?"

"Ah, well, I suppose I should explain a few things more fully while we have the benefit of privacy," he continued. "And don't mind the driver, he is safe.

"Back in the battle at Setauket in 1777, the owner of Penningcoll, an elderly Patriot man by the name of Mr. Jonas, was forced to flee to safer territory. He and I had exchanged a few business conversations, but of course you never met him. I had gotten to know his beliefs and more about the Patriot cause, and I began to sympathize with "the enemy," so to speak. Mr. Jonas knew he could not take the risk nor the time to sell the estate, so on his way off the island, he came to see me. He gave me the deed to his land and home in exchange for my promise to use his house as he had, as a safe house for couriers in the Culper Spy Ring. Of course, I couldn't betray his trust or my word, and so I did what I could to maintain the house for those who would come through."

"But how did you manage to keep this a secret from all of us?" I asked, trying to recall any times that may have given me a hint to the truth.

"That was getting increasingly difficult, so when events unfolded with Eric here," he gestured as he explained, "I was more than happy to give him a home as well as a task."

"So, you did the exact opposite of 'save him from his

rebelliousness' as the Kingsley's had hoped." I gave him a sly smile, and the four of us chuckled lightheartedly. "Tell me, though," I asked in seriousness of Eric, "do you think your relationship with your parents can ever be mended?"

He sighed deeply. "I certainly hope so, but even if it does not, I will rest easy knowing that I have done what God has asked me despite the loss of the approval of those close to me."

I gave him a compassionate and appreciative smile. "Well," I said, taking a breath, "I will not lie, that was quite a lot to discover all at once, but I am glad to be safely on our way home without secrets between us."

At that moment, we arrived at the small whaling boat that would take us back to Setauket without too much attention. We boarded quickly and took our seats on deck. This time I was seated beside my father, and Mr. Kingsley and Mr. Barlow sat across from us.

When we had settled and the boat had begun its crossing, my father again assumed a voice of seriousness and said, "Charlotte, I'm afraid we have still not told you everything." He glanced at Eric and then at Mr. Barlow, as if trying to decide whether or not to include them in this next divulgence. He appeared to determine it could do no harm, for he continued, "Mr. Jonas left more than his land and home, already sizable in value. He gave me the majority of his fortune as well. It has barely been tapped in all the doings at Penningcoll, and so, well, we are not so desolate as you and your mother and sister suppose. Of course, I had to keep the money a secret if I were to succeed in keeping its purpose a secret."

I breathed heavily, my head spinning with the implications of this revelation. Eric sensed my distress and offered his hand. I grasped it, hoping it would steady my nerves, but calm only returned when I looked into his eyes

IN THE WAITING

and saw there the love I now knew he had for me.

I turned back to Father and replied, "How? I mean, are you saying what I think you are?" "Yes, my sweet girl. I am. You have no need to marry money unless you truly do love the man." I saw how much it was hurting him to see how his secrets had hurt me. Our previous conversation in which I had assured him of my love for Lieutenant Taylor came back to me, and I could hold back the tears no longer. It would have played out quite differently if I had known then what I knew now.

"I'm sorry, Charlotte, but again, there is more." He looked, then, to Mr. Kingsley who continued the tale.

"When I came last autumn, your father did not feel right about keeping Mr. Jonas' wealth and land to himself when I was taking over much of the work he had been asked to do. In short, despite my pleas that being welcome at his home was payment enough, your father gave me the deed to Penningcoll, though I was able to convince him to keep the money."

This was getting to be too much to handle. "So, you are saying that *you* are the master of Penningcoll?"

He nodded hesitantly, watching for my reaction.

When I had comprehended what he was saying, I smiled. I didn't say a word, nor did I ask any more questions. I simply looked into those soft gray eyes and smiled in my delight. In only a moment I raised in station above the need to marry wealth, and he had risen from a nearly penniless prisoner of the British army to a free owner of a large estate. Everything between us had changed, and that wasn't a problem now, for there was the possibility now of something to come of the love we shared. I turned away then, for I did not want to get ahead of myself. We had much to face when we came home, and it was rather unlikely that Eric would be accepted into society again after all that had happened.

Chapter 25

Our somewhat tattered party arrived at Longford that evening. Andrew Barlow took his leave without entering the house, knowing what faced us when we were to enter. Mother and Mary Ann were still completely unaware of the truth about any of our dealings. We decided that now was as good a time as any and that they deserved to know what was going on. It was not going to be easy, but it was the right thing to do. Upon entering, floods of emotions swept over and around us all. My mother and sister were at first relieved to see Father and me, then bewildered to see Mr. Kingsley. Father would answer no questions but instead called all of us—Thomas, Mrs. Phillips, and Maggie included—into the drawing room for a detailed explanation of all that had transpired.

"I understand that what I have to say will be quite shocking," Father announced from his place in front of the hearth, "but I owe it to all of you to be forthright and no longer conceal what kind of business I am in."

His audience shifted uncomfortably and glanced around the room at each other.

"I am a Patriot, and Mr. Kingsley and I, with some help from Miss Devonshire, have been working for the cause of freedom for some time."

A death-like silence ensued for several minutes, but in one instant it was broken with utter chaos. After almost

IN THE WAITING

two hours of discussion, tears, anger, and several faints on the part of my mother, all the secrets came out and, rather surprisingly, all was forgiven and accepted. My mother was certainly more reluctant than Mary Ann, who after the initial shock thought Father and I were quite brave and heroic. Still, once Mother had a moment to consider and collect herself, as well as hear the truth about what the British had been doing, she was able to understand both why we had done what we did and why we had kept it a secret. I thought that, overall, it went surprisingly well.

With that ordeal over, I turned my thoughts to Lawrence, who, though I had become more than confident in the impossibility of our marriage, likely still believed I loved him and was planning to marry him as soon as he said the word.

A couple of days after our return, he finally paid us a visit. Thankfully, I was near the door when Thomas answered it, and so instead of taking him to see the rest of the household, I suggested we enjoy the fine day and take a walk down to the shore.

"I am sorry I have not been to see you for so long," he said as we started on our way, "I was rather busy."

"So I heard." It appeared Mother was right when she said she did not believe the Lieutenant knew of my absence from Longford. I was glad. I did not want to have to explain myself or lie about what I had been doing. There was no use conveying my sentiments about the war now. Our paths were diverging, and I could do more good if he were kept in the dark about some things. As Eric had said, I did not need to throw myself at the mercy of the law, I only needed to be willing to face it if ever the time came.

"In our brief time apart," I continued carefully, "I have had some time to think."

He looked down at me with expectation but said

nothing, so I waited a few moments to share what I had to say.

When we reached the beach, I stopped walking and turned to face Lawrence. I did not want to beat around the bush and so got straight to the point. "I cannot marry you," I said.

He gave a short, confused laugh before realizing I was in earnest. "You can't be serious," he said with a touch of frustration.

"I am afraid I am."

He spun away and took his hat into his fist. "Why?" he demanded, spinning back to face me.

"We could never have the kind of marriage we should. I see now that you do not truly love me anymore than I truly love you."

He rubbed a hand through his hair in bewilderment. He took a step towards me and grabbed my arm saying, "But I do! I have shown you I do!" He pulled me to him, but at that moment, something appeared in his view that made him release me, though not gently.

"If this is what you want, then so be it," he hissed. "You deserve a man like him," he nearly snarled. He looked behind me again before turning on his heel and storming away.

In shock I watched him leave, but with every increase in distance between us, relief and a new sense of freedom overcame me. I turned then towards where Lawrence had been looking and saw there Mr. Kingsley, now coming towards me.

"I hope you don't mind that I followed you. When I saw you leave with him, I just wanted to be sure you were safe."

I smiled. "Thank you, for everything."

He grinned back at me and offered his arm. "Shall we

return?" I nodded, but we did not hurry back.

～

I found out a few days later from Mary Ann, who found out through town gossip, what had become of the Lieutenant after storming off the way he had.

"Charlotte," she had begun cautiously after she had sat me down on my bedside, "I have some news, and though I know you are not attached to him anymore, I fear you will be quite distressed by what I have to say."

I prepared myself for what might be coming and answered, "Go on."

"Well, from what I gather, this is what seems to have happened after you…after your conversation with the Lieutenant. Sir Edward Barlow discovered Lieutenant Taylor with Ellen, kissing passionately…in her boudoir. Of course, Sir Edward ran him out of the house and scolded him fiercely above the brokenhearted sobs of Ellen, whom, I may add, has turned out to be much like her sister-in-law and a regrettably poor friend to me."

My blood boiled. "The scoundrel!" I exclaimed. "How could I have been so blind to his true character?"

"But that isn't even the end of the story," Mary Ann winced under the words. "Just this morning it has been discovered that he has run away with Ada Winters, likely to be married in New York among her more questionable friends."

I caught myself before saying some harsh words about the man (I shall no longer give him the title of gentleman), and instead took a deep breath. "They deserve each other," is all I said.

～

That night, after the evening meal, Mary Ann and our parents retired unusually early, leaving Mr. Kingsley and me in the drawing room to ourselves. The first thing he did was cross the room to open the double doors wide. I smiled to myself and thought how nice it was to have a true gentleman for company. He came and sat opposite my seat on the sofa.

"Eric." I was glad for the opportunity to tell him what I had wished to since hearing the news Mary Ann had shared. "You were right to distrust Lieutenant Taylor. As I am sure you have heard, he is a scoundrel, and I am ashamed to have fallen prey to his charms for so long."

He clenched his jaw in the usual way, only this time I saw for what reason he did. He could not stand the thought of me under the wiles of another man.

"I am sorry," I continued, "for not heeding your warnings." I hung my head.

He stood then and came to sit beside me, though not too close. "I only wanted to protect you, and I am afraid in large part I failed. I should have said more, done more."

I looked into his eyes and saw the pain of regret. "No, you are not to blame for how he used me."

He swallowed hard. There was awkward silence for a moment, and I stared at the floor. "May I give you your Christmas present?" he asked, changing the subject.

"But Christmas is more than five months away," I said, glad that conversation had resumed.

"Not this year's Christmas, last year's Christmas." I looked clearly confused.

"I never gave it to you. I almost did on Christmas morning, and I've had it with me ever since. Well, except for that time when my belongings were confiscated by the prison guard," he laughed lightly. "I never felt it was the right moment, and with your closeness to Lieutenant

IN THE WAITING

Taylor…"

I looked down sheepishly.

"But now, I believe, I might take the liberty of presenting it to you." He stood, touching my elbow so I would do the same, and placed the small box in my hand.

Our fingers brushed, and I took a sharp breath, struggling to keep from trembling as I stood just inches away from him. I began to open the tiny package. As I removed the lid, I gasped. It was not jewelry, as the wrapping suggested, but a folded, miniature American flag. "Oh! It's beautiful!"

He blushed and combed his fingers through his hair. "I'm afraid it might be rather ragged.

I am not as handy with a needle and thread as I know you are."

I noticed his allusion to my stitching Mr. Milton's leg, but let it pass with a smile. "You made this?"

He nodded.

"That is quite impressive."

His eyes shone. "At the time, I had wished to tell you the truth about my position and role with the colonial army. I felt I owed it to you. I wanted to give you something to remember me by, as I assumed I would have to leave with the way things were going between us and between you and the Lieutenant. But when Christmas morning came and we had our, well, we made our truce, dare I say, I thought perhaps I could stay and wait to reveal what I planned. But then, of course, the truth was shown when the Miltons first arrived."

I looked into the eyes of the man I had so severely misjudged. "Eric, how could I have been so blind? In all my waiting and hoping and dreaming for what the chapter of marriage would look like for me, I ignored all I had said I should look for in a man and refused to see it in you.

God sent you to me many months ago, and it has taken me this long to turn from the plans I had made for myself and instead follow the path He had paved for me."

His eyes shone with sweet tenderness. "Charlotte, darling Charlotte..." He tucked a wisp of hair behind my ear. "Would it be too presumptuous to ask..." He knelt before me. "Would you give me the greatest honor and pleasure and consent to be my wife?"

"Oh, Eric!" Feelings of completeness and joy washed over me. I hesitated, knowing the same feelings had betrayed me before, as I had felt this way when Lawrence first kissed me. But no, this was different. With the Lieutenant, all was spark and fire that merely simulated such feelings. With Eric, it was not his touch nor his attention or praise that inspired my happiness, but rather his promise to love me, care for me and guide me in the way I should go. That was enough to assure me that a life with him would be a life that would glorify God and satisfy even my deepest desires for fulfillment and purpose. Together we would strive for greatness in the service of the Father who had brought us together. "Yes!" I replied heartily. "With all my heart, yes!"

He rose and spun me around with a smile so bright even the coming shadows of evening held no darkness. When he set me down, he caught his breath, his face inches from mine. He whispered, "May I?"

I nodded slightly and closed my eyes.

His lips were sweet, like summer honey. I somehow knew at that moment that this honey would never run dry. I went limp, and his arms slid around my waist to hold me to him.

He released me, and a flash of harsh reality came back to me. "But I am not worthy of *you*," I said sorrowfully. "I am a disaster! You know what people say of me. It is still a wonder why a man like Lieutenant Taylor even wanted me. You are so far above all the men I've known before. I think you should be embarrassed to have me as a wife. After all, I have just broken an engagement, one I am ashamed to have ever been a part of." I looked down.

He reached out and lifted my chin till our eyes met. "You are worthy of people's good opinions. And when they don't see you the way I do… the way God does… well, it shouldn't matter. God has enough love to make up for any withheld from you by others, and I promise to add what love and care I can, regardless of what you think of yourself. Love is a gift, freely given from God to us… and from me to you."

I could not have kept my joy hidden if I had tried. "And from me to you," I promised in deep sincerity. I did not deserve this man, yet here he was, by God's grace.

Lawrence might have been a man of worth in one sense, but Eric was a man whose worth lay in his character and was infinitely more valuable. The wholeness I felt as he held me close was incomparable to the fleeting feelings that came with the Lieutenant. Eric loved me selflessly and sacrificially. I never could have expected to feel such joy with Lawrence. Here, with Eric, as he kissed me and whispered to me his undying love, my eyes were opened to what it would truly mean to have a husband who loved me. I felt sure nothing could wipe the smile from my face. I understood that though marriage is sometimes a duty, if it is truly good, it does more than soothe the pain of what one has given up. In fact, I *knew* my marriage would be better than anything I was giving up. It would be worth all the waiting.

Epilogue

It certainly was. Eric and I were married that autumn by Andrew Barlow, who officially became an ordained minister not long after our return from Connecticut. We fixed and cleaned Penningcoll and have lived there joyously for two years. The American Revolution was a success, and we now enjoy the freedoms for which we fought so hard.

We stayed out of society for most of the duration of the war but made wonderful memories with my parents and Mary Ann in the meantime. Mrs. Barlow, as well, came with her eldest son to visit often, and our party has become the closest of friends. In fact, I have a feeling Mr. Barlow may soon become more than a friend to Mary Ann.

As close as we are to my parents, it seems that it may still be some time before Eric's parents forgive him and accept me as their daughter-in-law. As we wait, we trust that God has us exactly where He wants us, and that He will be with us every step of the way.

I did find purpose in our work for the Culper Spy Ring, and I have also found purpose in being a wife, though not in the way I had expected. I love Eric, and being *his* wife is so much more than just being *a* wife. However, where I have found my true purpose is in neither of these roles. I am a daughter of God, and there is nothing that will ever change that.

Printed in the USA
CPSIA information can be obtained
at www.ICGtesting.com
LVHW021151310524
781582LV00010B/325